MASH

MASH

Richard Hooker

HARPER PERENNIAL

NEW YORK • LONDON • TORONTO • SYDNEY

HARPER ⬤ PERENNIAL

A hardcover edition of this book was published in 1968 by William Morrow.

MASH. Copyright © 1968, renewed 1996 by Richard Hornberger and W. C. Heinz. All rights reserved. Printed in the United States of America. No part of this book may be used or reproduced in any manner whatsoever without written permission except in the case of brief quotations embodied in critical articles and reviews. For information, address HarperCollins Publishers, 195 Broadway, New York, NY 10007.

HarperCollins books may be purchased for educational, business, or sales promotional use. For information, please e-mail the Special Markets Department at SPsales@harpercollins.com.

First Quill edition published 1997.

Reprinted in Perennial 2001.

Library of Congress Cataloging- the-Publication Data
Hooker, Richard.
    MASH / Richard Hooker.
    p. cm.
    ISBN 0-688-14955-3 (alk. paper)
    1. Korean War, 1950-1953—Medical care—Fiction. I. Title.
PS3558.O55M37   1997
813'.54—dc21   96-49064
                                                                                              CIP

23 24 25 26 27 LBC 38 37 36 35 34

Foreword

Most of the doctors who worked in Mobile Army Surgical Hospitals during the Korean War were very young, perhaps too young, to be doing what they were doing. They performed the definitive surgery on all the major casualties incurred by the 8th Army, the Republic of Korea Army, the Commonwealth Division and other United Nations forces. Helped by blood, antibiotics, helicopters, the tactical peculiarities of the Korean War and the youth and accompanying resiliency of their patients, they achieved the best results up to that time in the history of military surgery.

The surgeons in the MASH hospitals were exposed to extremes of hard work, leisure, tension, boredom, heat, cold, satisfaction and frustration that most of them had never faced before. Their reaction, individually and collectively, was to cope with the situation and get the job done. The various stresses, however, produced behavior in many of them that, superficially at least, seemed inconsistent with their earlier, civilian behavior patterns. A few flipped their lids, but most of them just raised hell, in a variety of ways

5

and degrees. This is a story of some of the ways and degrees. It's also a story of some of the work.

The characters in this book are composites of people I knew, met casually, worked with, or heard about. No one in the book bears more than a coincidental resemblance to an actual person.

MASH

1

When Radar O'Reilly, just out of high school, left Ottumwa, Iowa, and enlisted in the United States Army it was with the express purpose of making a career of the Signal Corps. Radar O'Reilly was only five feet three inches tall, but he had a long, thin neck and large ears that left his head at perfect right angles. Furthermore, under certain atmospheric, as well as metabolic, conditions, and by enforcing complete concentration and invoking unique extra-sensory powers, he was able to receive messages and monitor conversations far beyond the usual range of human hearing.

With this to his advantage it seemed to Radar O'Reilly that he was a natural for the communications branch of the service, and so, following graduation, he turned down various highly attractive business opportunities, some of them legitimate, and decided to serve his country. Before his enlistment, in fact, he used to fall asleep at night watching a whole succession of, first, sleeve stripes, and then shoulder insignia, floating by until he would see himself, with four stars on his shoulders, conducting high-level Pentagon brief-

9

ings, attending White House dinner parties and striding imperiously to ringside tables in New York night clubs.

In the middle of November of the year 1951 A.D., Radar O'Reilly, a corporal in the United States Army Medical Corps, was sitting in the Painless Polish Poker and Dental Clinic of the 4077th Mobile Army Surgical Hospital astride the 38th Parallel in South Korea, ostensibly trying to fill a straight flush. Having received the message that the odds against such a fortuitous occurrence open at 72,192 to 1, what he was actually doing was monitoring a telephone conversation. The conversation was being conducted, over a precarious connection, between Brigadier General Hamilton Hartington Hammond, the Big Medical General forty-five miles to the south in Seoul, and Lieutenant Colonel Henry Braymore Blake, in the office of the commanding officer of the 4077th MASH, just forty-five yards to Radar O'Reilly's east.

"Listen," Radar O'Reilly said, his head turning slowly back and forth in the familiar scanning action.

"Listen to what?" Captain Walter Koskiusko Waldowski, the Dental Officer and Painless Pole, asked.

"Henry," Radar O'Reilly said, "is trying for two new cutters."

"I gotta have two more men," Colonel Blake was shouting into the phone, and Radar could hear it.

"What do you think you're running up there?" General Hammond was shouting back, and Radar could hear that, too. "Walter Reed Hospital?"

"Now you listen to me . . ." Colonel Blake was saying.

"Just take it easy, Henry," General Hammond was saying.

"I won't take it easy," Colonel Blake shouted. "If I don't get two . . ."

"All right! All right!" General Hammond shouted. "So I'll send you the two best men I have."

10

"They better be good," Radar heard Colonel Blake answer, "or I'll . . ."

"I said they'll be the two best men I've got," Radar heard General Hammond say.

"Good!" Radar heard Colonel Blake say. "And get 'em here quick."

"Henry," Radar said, his ears aglow now from the activity, "has just got us two new cutters."

"Tell 'em not to spend it all before they get here," Captain Waldowski said. "You want another card?"

Thus it was that the personnel of the 4077th MASH learned that their number, and perhaps even their efficiency, would shortly be augmented. Thus it was that, on a gray, raw morning ten days later at the 325th Evacuation Hospital in Yong-Dong-Po, across the Han River from Seoul, Captains Augustus Bedford Forrest and Benjamin Franklin Pierce, emerging from opposite ends of the Transient Officer's Quarters, dragged themselves, each hauling a Valpac and trailing a barracks bag, toward a jeep deposited there for their use.

Captain Pierce was twenty-eight years old, slightly over six feet tall and slightly stoop-shouldered. He wore glasses, and his brown-blond hair needed cutting. Captain Forrest was a year older, slightly under six feet tall, and more solid. He had brush-cut red hair, pale blue eyes and a nose that had not quite been restored to its natural state after contact with something more resistant than itself.

"You the guy going to the 4077th?" Captain Pierce said to Captain Forrest as they confronted each other at the jeep.

"I believe so," Captain Forrest said.

"Then get in," Captain Pierce said.

"Who drives?" Captain Forrest said.

"Let's choose," Captain Pierce said. He opened his barracks bag, felt around in it and extracted a Stan Hack model Louisville Slugger. He handed the bat to Captain Forrest.

"Toss," he said.

11

Captain Forrest tossed the bat vertically into the air. As it came down Captain Pierce expertly grabbed it at the tape with his left hand. Captain Forrest placed his left hand above Captain Pierce's. Captain Pierce placed his right hand, and Captain Forrest was left with his right hand waving in the air with nothing to grab.

"Sorry," Captain Pierce said. "Always use your own bat."

That was all he said. They got into the jeep and for the first five miles they did not speak again, until Captain Forrest broke the silence.

"What are y'all anyway?" Captain Forrest asked. "A nut?"

"It's likely," Captain Pierce said.

"My name's Duke Forrest. Who are y'all?"

"Hawkeye Pierce."

"Hawkeye Pierce?" Captain Forrest said. "What the hell kind of a name is that?"

"The only book my old man ever read was *The Last of the Mohicans*," Captain Pierce explained.

"Oh," Captain Forrest said, and then: "Where y'all from?"

"Crabapple Cove."

"Where in hell is that?"

"Maine," Hawkeye said. "Where you from?"

"Forrest City."

"Where in hell is that?"

"Georgia," Duke said.

"Jesus," Hawkeye said. "I need a drink."

"I got some," Duke said.

"Make it yourself, or is it real?" Hawkeye asked.

"Where I come from it's real if you make it yourself," Duke Forrest said, "but I bought this from the Yankee government."

"Then I'll try it."

Captain Pierce pulled to the side of the road and stopped the jeep. Captain Forrest found the pint in his barracks bag and opened it. As they sat there, looking down the road, flanked by the rice paddies skimmed now with November ice, they passed the bottle back and forth and talked.

Duke Forrest learned that Hawkeye Pierce was married and the father of two young sons, and Captain Pierce found out that Captain Forrest was married and the father of two young girls. They discovered that their training and experience had been remarkably similar and each detected, with much relief, that the other did not think of himself as a Great Surgeon.

"Hawkeye," Captain Forrest said after a while. "Do y'all realize that this is amazing?"

"What's amazing?"

"I mean, I come from Forrest City, Georgia, and y'all are a Yankee from that Horseapple . . ."

"Crabapple."

". . . Crabapple Cove in Maine, and we've got so much in common."

"Duke," Hawkeye said, holding up the bottle and noting that its contents were more than half depleted, "we haven't got as much of this in common as we used to."

"Then maybe we'd better push on," the Duke said.

As they drove north, only the sound of the jeep breaking the silence, a cold rain started to fall, almost obscuring the jagged, nearly bare hills on either side of the valley. They came to Ouijongbu, a squalid shanty town with a muddy main street lined with tourist attractions, the most prominent of which, at the northern outskirts, was The Famous Curb Service Whorehouse.

The Famous Curb Service Whorehouse, advantageously placed as it was on the only major highway between Seoul and the front lines, had the reputation of being very good because all the truck drivers stopped there. It was unique for its methods of merchandising and outstanding for its contribution to the venereal disease problem faced by the U.S. Army Medical Corps. It consisted of a half dozen mud and thatch huts, prefaced by a sign reading: "Last Chance Before Peking" and surmounted by an American flag flying from its central edifice. Its beckoning personnel, clad in the most colorful ensembles available through the Sears Roebuck catalogue, lined the highway regardless of the weather, and many drivers who made frequent trips to the front and back fastidiously found their fulfillment in the backs of their trucks, rather than expose themselves to the dirty straw and soiled mattresses indoors.

"You need anything here?" asked Hawkeye, noting the Duke saluting and nodding as the jeep chugged through the waving, cooing colorama.

"No," the Duke said. "I shopped in Seoul last night, but something else bothers me now."

"You should know better, doctor," Hawkeye said.

"No," Duke said. "I've been wondering about this Colonel Blake."

"Lieutenant Colonel Henry Braymore Blake," Hawkeye said. "I looked him up. Regular Army type."

"You need a drink?" Duke said.

Out of sight of the sirens now, Hawkeye pulled the jeep to the side of the road once more. By the time they had finished the bottle the cold, slanting rain was mixed with flat wet flakes of snow.

"Regular Army type," the Duke kept repeating. "Like Meade and Sherman and Grant."

"The way I see it, though, is this," Hawkeye said, finally. "Most of these Regular Army types are insecure. If they weren't, they'd take their chances out in the big free world. Their only security is based on the efficiency of their outfits."

"Right," the Duke said.

"This Blake must have a problem or he wouldn't be sending for help. Maybe we're that help."

"Right," the Duke said.

14

"So my idea," Hawkeye said, "is that we work like hell when there's work and try to outclass the other talent."

"Right," the Duke said.

"This," Hawkeye said, "will give us enough leverage to write our own tickets the rest of the way."

"Y'all know something, Hawkeye?" the Duke said. "You're a good man."

Just beyond a collection of tents identified as the Canadian Field Dressing Station, they came to a fork in the road. The road to the right led northeast toward the Punchbowl and Heartbreak Ridge; the road to the left took them due north toward Chorwon, Pork Chop Hill, Old Baldy and the 4077th MASH.

About four miles beyond the fork, a flooded stream had washed out a bridge, and a couple of M.P.'s waved them into a line with a dozen other military vehicles, including two tanks. They waited there for an hour, the line lengthening behind them until the line ahead began to move and Hawkeye guided the jeep down the muddy river bank and across the floorboard-deep stream.

As a result, darkness was settling on the valley when, opposite a sign that read "THIS IS WHERE IT IS—PARALLEL 38," another, smaller marker reading "4077th MASH, WHERE I AM, HENRY BLAKE, LT. COL. M.C." directed them to the left off the main road. Following directions, they were confronted, first, by four helicopters belonging to the 5th Air Rescue Squadron and then by several dozen tents of various shapes and sizes, forlornly distributed in the shape of a horseshoe.

"Well," Hawkeye said, stopping the jeep, "there it is."

"Damn," Duke said.

The rain had changed to wet snow by now, and off the muddy road the ground was white. With the motor idling, they could hear the rumble of artillery.

"Thunder?" Duke said.

"Man-made," Hawkeye said. "They welcome all newcomers this way."

"What do we do now?" Duke said.

"Find the mess hall," Hawkeye said. "It figures to be that thing over there."

When they walked into the mess hall there were about a dozen others sitting at one of the long, rectangular tables. They chose an unoccupied table, sat down, and were served by a Korean boy wearing green fatigue pants and an off-white coat.

As they ate they knew they were being looked over. Finally one of the others got up and approached them. He was about five feet eight, a little overweight, a little red of face and eye, and balding. On the wings of his shirt collar were silver oak leaves, and he looked worried.

"I'm Colonel Blake," he said, eyeing them. "You fellows just passing through?"

"No," replied Hawkeye. "We're assigned here."

"You sure?" the Colonel asked.

"Y'all said you all needed two good boys," Duke said, "and we're what the Army sent."

"Where you guys been all day? I expected you by noon."

"We stopped at a gin mill," the Duke told him.

"Let me see your orders."

They got out their papers and handed them to the Colonel. They watched him while he checked the papers and then while he eyed the two of them again.

"Well, it figures," Henry said finally. "You guys look like a pair of weirdos to me, but if you work well I'll hold still for a lot and if you don't it's gonna be your asses."

"You see?" Hawkeye said to Duke. "I told you."

"You're a good man," Duke said.

"Colonel," Hawkeye said, "have no fear. The Duke and Hawkeye are here."

"You'll know you're here by morning," Henry said. "You go

16

to work at nine o'clock tonight, and I just got word that the gooks have hit Kelly Hill."

"We're ready," Hawkeye said.

"Right," Duke said.

"You're living with Major Hobson," Henry said. "O'Reilly?"

"Sir?" Radar O'Reilly said, already at the Colonel's side, for he had received the message even before it had been sent.

"Don't do that, O'Reilly," Henry said. "You make me nervous."

"Sir?"

"Take these officers . . ."

"To Major Hobson's tent," Radar said.

"Stop that, O'Reilly," Henry said.

"Sir?"

"Oh, get out of here," Henry said.

Thus it came about that it was Radar O'Reilly, who had been the first to know they were coming, who led Captains Pierce and Forrest to their new home. At the moment, Major Hobson was out, so Hawkeye and Duke each selected a sack and lay down. They were just dropping off to sleep when the door opened.

"Welcome, fellows," a voice boomed, followed by a medium-sized major, who entered with a warm smile and offered a firm handshake.

Major Hobson was thirty-five years old. He had practiced a good deal of general medicine, a little surgery, and every Sunday he had preached in the Church of the Nazarene in a small midwestern town. The fortunes of war had given him a job for which he was unprepared, and associated him with people he could not comprehend.

"You fellows certainly are welcome," he intoned. "Would you like to look around the outfit?"

"No," said Duke. "We been stoned all day. Guess we'll get a little sleep."

"We've gotta fix the President's hernia at nine o'clock,"

Hawkeye said. "We're Harry's family surgeons. We'd ask you to assist, but the Secret Service is worried about Chinese agents."

"Yankee Chinks from the north," Duke said. "Y'all understand."

Jonathan Hobson was shocked and confused, and there was much he didn't understand. Soon after nine o'clock he understood even less. The gooks had indeed hit Kelly Hill, the casualties were rolling in, and the five men on the 9:00 P.M. to 9:00 A.M. shift had their hands full.

When 9:00 A.M. arrived, it was clear that the most and best work had been done by Hawkeye Pierce and Duke Forrest. Among other things, the two, functioning as if they had been working across the table from each other for years, did two bowel resections, which means removing a piece of bowel damaged by such foreign bodies as fragments of shells and mines. Then they did a thoracotomy for control of hemorrhage, which means they opened a chest to stop the bleeding caused by the entrance of a similar body, and they topped this off by removing a lacerated spleen and a destroyed kidney from the same patient.

The ease with which they handled these and several more minor cases naturally stimulated considerable comment and speculation about them. With their chores done, however, Hawkeye and Duke were too tired to care, and right after breakfast they headed across the compound for Tent Six.

As the components of the 4077th MASH were arranged around the horseshoe, the operating tent, with its tin Quonset roof, was in the middle of the closed end. The admitting ward and laboratory were to the left and the postop ward to the right. Next to the laboratory was the Painless Polish Poker and Dental Clinic, then the mess hall, the PX, the shower tent, the barber shop, and the enlisted men's tents. On the other side, and strung out from the postop ward, were the tents where the officers lived, then nurse country, and finally the quarters for the Korean hired hands. Fifty yards beyond these domiciles was a lonely tent on the edge of a mine field. This was the Officers' Club. If one walked carefully and obliquely northwesterly for another seventy-five yards beyond the Officers' Club and didn't fall into old bunkers, he'd reach a high bank overlooking a wide, usually shallow, branch of the Imjin River.

"Southern boy," Hawkeye was saying as they approached their tent, "I'm going to have myself a butt and a large shot of tax-free GI booze and hit the sack."

"I'm with y'all," Duke was saying, as Hawkeye opened the door affixed to the front of the tent.

"Look!" Hawkeye said.

Duke looked where Hawkeye was pointing. In one corner, kneeling on the dirt floor with his elbows on his cot, a Bible in front of him, his lips moving slowly, and oblivious to all about him, was Major Jonathan Hobson.

"Jesus," Hawkeye said.

"It don't look like Him," Duke said.

"Do you think he's gone ape?"

"Naw," Duke said. "I think he's a Roller. We got lots of them back home."

"We've got some back at the Cove, too," Hawkeye said. "You've gotta watch 'em."

"Y'all watch him," Duke said. "It would bore me."

While Major Hobson maintained his position, they had a large drink and then one more. Then, in loud, unmelodious voices, they sang as much as they could remember of "Onward Christian Soldiers" and crawled exhausted into their sleeping bags.

When they awoke, darkness had come again, and so had another load of casualties. The casualties continued to pour in without letup for a whole week, and the new surgeons did more than their share of the work. This naturally aroused a growing respect among their colleagues, but it was respect mixed with doubt and wonder, for they fitted no recognizable pattern.

2

Nine days after the arrival of Captains Pierce and Forrest at the Double Natural, as the 4077th was called by the resident crapshooters, two things happened. There came a lull in business, and the shifts changed so that the two were working days. Both men much preferred this combination of circumstances except that now, each morning as they arose for breakfast, they were forced to witness and walk around their tentmate, Major Jonathan Hobson, kneeling in prayer beside his cot.

"Major," said Hawkeye one morning, as the lengthy ritual came to an end, "you seem to be somewhat preoccupied with religion. Are you on this kick for good, or is this just a passing fancy?"

"Make fun of me all you want," replied the Major, "but I'll continue to pray, particularly for you and Captain Forrest."

"Why, y'all . . ." the Duke started to say.

Hawkeye broke him off. It was obvious that the Duke did not wish to accept salvation from a Yankee evangelist, so Hawkeye motioned him to follow and they left the tent.

"Let's get rid of him," the Duke said, when they were out-side. "I don't like that man, and he's stuntin' our social growth, too."

"I know," Hawkeye agreed. "He's such a simple clunk that I kind of hate to roust him, but I can't put up with him, either."

"What are we gonna do?" Duke said.

"We are going to ditch the Major," Hawkeye said, "but let's be quiet about it. No use kicking up too much of a fuss."

Hawkeye and Duke knocked on the door of Colonel Blake's tent and were told to enter. After they had made themselves comfortable, Hawkeye opened the conversation.

"How are you today, Colonel?" he said.

"That's not what you two came to ask," the Colonel said, eyeing them.

"Well, Henry," Hawkeye said, "we don't wish to cause any trouble, but we strongly suspect that something that might embarrass this excellent organization could occur if you don't get that sky pilot out of our tent."

"*Your* tent?" Henry started to say, and then he thought better of it. He sat there in silence for almost a minute, while the surge and counter-surge of his emotions played across the red of his face in iridescent waves.

"I have been in this Army a long time," he said finally, measuring his words. "I know just what you guys are up to. You figure you have me over a barrel, and to a certain extent you do. You do your jobs very well. We're going to lose our other experienced men and get a bunch of greenhorn replace-ments. You two are essential, but you can hold me up for just so much. If I go along with you now, where is it going to end?"

"Colonel," Hawkeye said, "we appreciate your position."

"Right," Duke said.

"I will define ours," Hawkeye said. "It reads about like this: As long as we are here we are going to do the best job we can. When the work comes our way we will do all in our power to promote the surgical efficiency of the outfit because that's what we hired out for."

"Right," Duke said.

"We'll also show reasonable respect for you and your job, but you may have to put up with a few things from us that haven't been routine around here. We don't think it will be anything you can't stand, but if it is you'll just have to get rid of us in any way you can."

"Boys," said the Colonel, after a moment's reflection, "I'm not sure what I'm getting into, but Hobson will be out of your tent today."

He reached under his cot and came up with three cans of beer.

"Have a beer," he said.

"Why, thank y'all," Duke said.

"Then there's one other small thing," Hawkeye said.

"What's that?" the Duke said to Hawkeye.

"The chest-cutter," Hawkeye said to the Duke.

"Yeah," Duke said to the Colonel.

"What?" the Colonel said.

During the quiet period that had settled upon the western Korean front, few shots had been fired in anger, and the only casualties had resulted from jeep accidents and from soldiers invading mine fields in search of pheasant and deer. Hawkeye and Duke had handled the lower extremity and abdominal damage of the hunters with their customary ease. When it came, however, to the depressed fractures of the sternum and multiple broken ribs with attendant complications sustained by the jeep jockeys, they both wished that they had had more formal training in chest surgery.

"That's right," Duke said to the Colonel. "Y'all better get us a chest-cutter."

"Stop dreaming," Henry said, "and drink your beer."

"We've been thinking," Hawkeye said, "that maybe you

could trade two or three of these Medical Service clowns around here for somebody who can find his way around the pulmonary anatomy when the bases are loaded . . ."

". . . And it's the ninth inning," Duke said.

"Listen," Henry said. "I'll give it to you just the way the General would give it to me. Do you guys think this is Walter Reed? You're doing fine."

"We are like hell," Hawkeye said. "We're swinging with our eyes closed, and . . ."

". . . and up to now we've just been lucky," Duke said.

"Forget it," Henry said. "How's the beer?"

"Forget it, hell," Hawkeye said. "You're evading the issue. We have more chest trauma right here than any hospital at home and we need somebody who really knows how to take care of it. We're learning, but not enough. You know that, just as well as we do."

"That's right," Duke said.

"Forget it," Henry said, "and by the way, with Hobson out of your tent as of now, please put in a little time for him in the preop ward."

It had long been customary at the 4077th for the surgeons on duty to spend their time, when not called upon to operate, in the preoperative ward. On quiet days this was unnecessary. The arrival of casualties was always known in advance, no one could get more than three hundred yards away, and thus each doctor was available in minutes.

The logic of this had never gotten through to Major Hobson, however, and as titular head of the day shift he had attempted to impose the useless vigil upon Captains Pierce and Forrest as soon as they had joined his section. Hawkeye and the Duke had failed to comply, letting it be known that they would usually be available at the poker game that ran perpetually in the Painless Polish Poker and Dental Clinic, where Captain Waldowski, of Hamtramck, Michigan, and

24

the Army Dental Corps, supplied cards, beer and painless extraction for all comers, twenty-four hours a day.

"I don't know, Henry," Hawkeye said now. "That's asking a lot, but if you get us that chest-cutter . . ."

"Get out of here!" Henry said. "Just finish your beers and get out of here!"

When not in the poker game, Hawkeye and Duke were likely to be in their tent. That very afternoon, shortly after lunch while all was quiet, Hawkeye was in the game, but Duke was in what was now their private quarters, propped up on his cot, a writing tablet on his knees. Every day he faithfully wrote his wife, a very time-consuming procedure, and he was thus engaged when Major Hobson came charging into the tent and demanded that Captain Forrest come to the preoperative ward immediately.

"Are there any patients?" Duke asked.

"That's neither here nor there," the Major replied austerely.

"If there ain't no patients there I stay here."

"Come to the preoperative ward immediately!" yelled the Major. "That's a direct order!"

"Y'all get out of here," was Duke's quiet answer.

The Major advanced like an avenging angel. The Duke came off his sack like the Georgia fullback he had once been, and Major Jonathan Hobson found himself prostrate in the snow and slush six feet from the tent door.

"That, you ridiculous rebel," said Hawkeye when he heard about it and got back to the tent, "was about as bright as Pickett's Charge. This will be trouble."

The expected arrival of Colonel Blake was forthcoming within minutes. The door opened, Colonel Blake entered, and the door slammed shut behind him.

"You guys have had it!" he shouted, purple-faced and suffused with military indignation. "I'm having you court-martialed!"

"Henry," said Hawkeye, "I had nothing to do with it. It

25

was all this dumb southern boy. However, I'll gladly partici-
pate in the consequences. Where do we get court-martialed?
Tokyo, or maybe San Francisco?"

"San Francisco, hell. You get court-martialed here and
now. You're both confined to the post for one month. This
is a summary court-martial, and I've just held it."

"But y'all can't . . ." the Duke started to say.

"Look, Henry," Hawkeye said, "be reasonable. I wouldn't
know how to get off this post if I wanted to, but I'd like to
keep the way open in case they make me Surgeon General
of the United States."

"Me too," Duke said.

With a grunt, the commanding officer departed, and it is
possible that the penalty would have stood, except that the
very next day Major Hobson, his ego restored and perhaps
even enlarged by the Colonel's legal action, extended his
activities. He began praying in the mess hall for fifteen
minutes before each meal.

"That'll do it," Hawkeye predicted to the Duke.

It did. Colonel Henry Blake was endowed with more
human understanding than is required of a Regular Army
Medical Officer, but after three days of this he left his lunch
uneaten, went to his tent, called 8th Army Headquarters,
arranged orders for Major Hobson, drove him to Seoul and
put him on a plane for Tokyo and home where, a few weeks
later, the Major's enlistment would expire. Honorably dis-
charged, he would return to his general practice, his occasional excursions into minor surgery and his church.

Returning from Seoul on the night of his Great Delivery,
Colonel Blake was very tired and slightly mulled, but he
mixed himself a drink and then collapsed on his cot. Before
he could find sleep, however, Hawkeye Pierce and Duke
Forrest entered. Apparently contrite, they silently helped
themselves to a drink. Then they knelt in front of their commanding officer and started to pray.

"Lordy, Lordy, Colonel, Sir," they wailed, "send our asses home."

"Get your asses out of here!" yelled Colonel Blake, rising in wrath.

"Yes, sir!" they said, salaaming as they went.

3 Several weeks after the departure of Major
Hobson, it was against first reported by Radar
O'Reilly and then announced by Colonel Blake that a new
surgeon had been assigned to the 4077th MASH. The only
available information was that he was a chest surgeon and
he was from Boston.

"Great!" exulted Hawkeye.

"Goddam Yankee," said Duke.

"Undoubtedly a good boy," said Hawkeye.

He arrived on a cold and snowy morning about nine
o'clock. Henry brought him to the mess hall for coffee and
introduced him to the other surgeons, most of whom, because
the gooks had been quiet for three days, were there.

The new boy was six feet tall and weighed about a hundred and thirty pounds. His name was John McIntyre. The
fatigue suit and parka he wore prevented anyone from getting much of a look at him. He acknowledged introductions
with noncommittal grunts, he sat down at a table, pulled a
can of beer out of a pocket and opened it. Then his head dis-

appeared into the parka like a turtle's into its shell, and the beer followed it.

"Seems like a nice fella," Duke said, "for a Yankee."

"Where you from, Dr. McIntyre?" someone asked.

"Winchester."

"Where did you go to school?"

"Winchester High," from somewhere inside the parka.

"I mean medical school."

"I forget, I guess."

"That," said Hawkeye to the Duke, "ought to stop the conversation for a while. I got a feeling I've seen this thing before. Wish he'd come out of the cocoon."

Captain Ugly John Black, the chief anesthesiologist, apparently decided to smoke him out. During his long working hours, when operating-room technique required that the anesthesiologist attending the patient be separated from the rest of the operating team, Ugly John was often lonesome for conversation. The new man's laconic responses were at least more talk than Ugly John could get back from his anesthetized patients.

"Have a good trip over?" he asked.

"Nope."

"Fly?"

"Nope."

Ugly scratched his head and figured he'd play the guy's own game.

"So what did you do, walk?"

"Yep."

"Great idea," Ugly said. "I wonder why I didn't think of it."

The head came out of the parka and looked Ugly over with great care.

"I don't know," it said.

By now it seemed fairly obvious to the group that they had some kind of a nut on their hands, and all, including Duke and Hawkeye, departed with haste. During the day, while the new boy was being oriented and supplied with this and that, most of the outfit went to Henry and asked him not to put Captain McIntyre in any of their tents—all except Duke and Hawkeye.

"Let's see what happens," Hawkeye said.

"Yeah," Duke said.

Late that afternoon it happened. The door of the tent swung open, and in came the new boy, bag and baggage. The baggage was dumped on one of the empty cots, and the new boy lay down. A hand went into the depths of the parka, came out with a can of beer, went back in and came out with an opener. The new boy opened the beer, and for the first time he looked at his new tentmates.

"It's a small place," he said, "but I think I'm going to love it."

"My name's Pierce, and this is Duke Forrest," Hawkeye said, getting up and offering his hand.

The newcomer didn't budge.

"Seen you before, haven't I?" asked Hawkeye.

"I don't know. Have you?" answered McIntyre.

"For Chrissake, McIntyre, are you all this friendly all the time?" demanded the Duke.

"Only when I'm happy," answered McIntyre.

Hawkeye went out, filled a bucket with snow and mixed martinis. He poured two, thought a moment, shrugged his shoulders, and asked the new boy if he would like one.

"Yep. Got any olives?"

"No."

The hand disappeared into the parka and came out with a bottle of olives. An olive was removed and placed in the martini.

"You guys want an olive?"

"Yeah."

An olive was doled out to each. The Duke gave a contented sigh.

"McIntyre," he said, "you're a regular perambulatin' PX."

Hawkeye laughed loudly. The martini and the head came out of the parka, looked at him, then disappeared again.

Duke and Hawkeye were on night duty, and the new boy was assigned to their shift. A Canadian unit had spent the day getting shot up a few miles to the west, so the night was a busy one, and there were several chest wounds. About all Duke or Hawkeye or anyone else at the Double Natural knew about the chest was what they had learned by bitter and difficult experience in recent weeks. The new boy didn't say much, but he did come out of the parka and show them what to do.

In the third chest that he opened he went right to and repaired a lacerated pulmonary artery, and he did it like Joe D. going back for a routine fly. When morning came the night shift went to the mess hall, their curiosity aroused more than ever by the new chest surgeon from Boston. At breakfast, another can of beer materialized from the recesses of the parka and, once opened, disappeared back into it.

At the Double Natural a rag-tag squad of Korean kids waited on tables, and one of them placed a bowl of oatmeal and a cup of coffee in front of Dr. McIntyre. The head shot out of the parka, and two glaring eyes focused on the boy.

"What's that?"

"Oatmeals, sir."

"I don't want oatmeals. Bring me bean."

"Bean hava no."

"OK. The hell with it."

Breakfast was quiet after that, and, as soon as the three had made it back to Tent Number Six, they went to bed, the new boy still in his parka.

At 4:00 P.M., Duke and Hawkeye got up, dressed and washed. From deep down in the parka, which had shown no previous signs of life, came the words:

"How about a martini?"

Hawkeye mixed, and again the olives were produced. After the first martini the new boy got up, took off the parka for the first time, washed his face, combed his hair, and got back into the parka. This look at him confirmed the impression Duke had formed the night before in the OR that Dr. McIntyre was about as thin as a man could get, and for the second time he addressed his new associate.

"Hey, boy, y'all got the clap?"

An immediate answer was not forthcoming. The head did come out of the parka, however, and look vaguely interested.

"What in hell makes you think he's got the clap?" Hawkeye asked. "Even a clap doctor can't diagnose it through a parka."

"What y'all don't know," replied Duke, "is that I'm a graduate of the Army Medical Field Service School at Fort Sam Houston, Texas, where I won high honors. I learned that the only thing that can go wrong with a soldier is for him to get shot or get the clap. He ain't bleeding so he's gotta have the clap."

"Well, when you put it that way," Hawkeye said, "it does make sense. However, he may be an exception to the rule."

"I don't have the clap," said the parka.

"See? What did I tell you?" said Hawkeye.

In the days that followed, John McIntyre continued to be an enigma. He and Hawkeye Pierce talked a little and looked each other over a little, and Hawkeye continued to have the nagging thought that he had seen him somewhere before.

One afternoon, about a week after the new doctor's arrival, with the snow temporarily gone, some of the boys were throwing a football around. As Hawkeye and McIntyre emerged from their tent, a wild throw brought the ball to rest at the latter's feet. He leaned over very, very slowly and picked up the ball. With a lazy wave of his hand he motioned Hawkeye downfield. When the Hawk was thirty yards off, McIntyre whipped a perfect pass into his arms. They continued their walk to the mess hall in silence, but Hawkeye was bothered again by memories he couldn't quite bring into focus.

"Where'd you go to college, John?" he asked over a cup of coffee.

"It was a small place, but I loved it. Where'd you go?"

"Androscoggin."

McIntyre grinned, but he didn't say anything.

By midafternoon it had started to snow again. The Duke, between complaints about the Yankee weather, was writing his wife, and Hawkeye was reading *The Maine Coast Fisherman* when McIntyre got up from his cot and headed for the door.

"Where you goin'?" asked Hawk.

"To the Winter Carnival."

With that he headed out of the tent in the general direction of the mountain to the west. Half an hour later he was seen halfway up it.

"That," said Duke Forrest, "is the strangest son-of-a-bitch I ever did see. If he wasn't the best chest-cutter in the Far East Command, I'd kick his ass out of this here tent."

"Just wait," Hawkeye said.

Martini time came. Duke and Hawkeye were having their first, Hawkeye deep in thought.

"I know I've seen that guy before," he said finally, "and before long I'm going to remember where. I figure he went to Dartmouth, with all this Winter Carnival crap. Also Daniel Webster said, 'It's a small place,' and so forth. Which reminds me, did I ever tell you how I beat Dartmouth single-handed?"

"Yeah, but only sixteen times. Tell me again."

"Well, it was just a midseason breather for the Big Green, but a blizzard blew up and it was 0–0 going into the last minute. They had this boy who was supposed to be a great passer so he threw one, snow and all, and—"

Just then the door opened, and in came McIntyre covered with snow.

"Where's the martinis?" he asked.

33

Hawkeye looked at him, and suddenly the intervening years and the nine thousand miles dissolved and memory functioned. Perhaps it was the snow or the thought of Dartmouth or both. He jumped up.

"Jesus to Jesus and eight hands around, Duke!" he yelled. "You know who we been living with for the past week? We been living with the only man in history who ever took a piece in the ladies' can of a Boston & Maine train. When the conductor caught him in there with his Winter Carnival date she screamed, 'He trapped me!' and that's how he got his name. This is the famous Trapper John. God, Trapper, I speak for the Duke as well as myself when I say it's an honor to have you with us. Have a martini, Trapper."

"Thanks, Hawkeye. I wondered when you'd recognize me. The minute I saw you I knew you were the guy that intercepted that pass. Lucky you didn't have your mouth open or it would have gone down your throat."

"Trapper, Trapper, Trapper," Hawkeye kept saying, and shaking his head. "Say, what you been doing since then?"

"Not much. Just living on my reputation."

The Duke got up and shook hands with Trapper.

"Right proud to know y'all, Trapper," he said. "Are you sure y'all don't have the clap? Y'all look right peaked."

"I got over the clap. I'm so skinny because I don't eat."

"Why not?"

"Got out of the habit."

"Don't let it worry you," Hawkeye said.

"It could happen to anybody," Duke said.

And so the Trapper was one of them. An hour later the three tentmates weaved into the mess hall, arm in arm.

"Gentlemen," yelled Hawkeye, "this here is Trapper John, the pride of Winchester, Dartmouth College, and Tent Number Six, and if any of you uneducated bastards don't like it you'll have to answer to Duke Forrest and Hawkeye Pierce."

4 For several weeks following the identification of Captain John McIntyre as Trapper John things settled down into an orderly routine. The work during the twelve-hour shifts was often intense, sometimes lacking, and usually somewhere in between.

Although many of the casualties were brought in from the Battalion Aid Stations by ambulance and might arrive at any hour, the most seriously wounded were flown in by helicopter. This meant that daylight was the frequent arrival time because the choppers did not fly at night. When the night shift had worked steadily from 9:00 P.M. to 4:00 A.M. and finally had everything cleaned up, some of its members could usually be seen as the first light of day seeped into the wide valley, peering north beyond the mine field and the river with its railroad bridge, hoping against hope that no choppers would materialize out of the mist.

When casualties were heavy, the regular schedule was ignored and every man worked as long as he could stay on his feet, think and still function. Finally, overcome by fatigue, he would grab a few hours of sleep and then go back to it again. When things were under control, however, there was leisure time and, particularly in winter and early spring, very little to do with it.

Tent Number Six, the home of Forrest, Pierce and McIntyre, became a center of social activity. It also became known as The Swamp, partly because it looked like the kind of haunt one might come across in a bog and partly because Hawkeye Pierce, while in college and unable to afford a dormitory room, had lived just off the campus in a shanty that his classmates had called The Swamp. The words, in big capital letters—THE SWAMP—were painted in red on the door of Number Six.

Cocktail hour at The Swamp began at 4:00 P.M., the hour at which the night shift normally awakened and had a few before supper, and the hour at which the day shift, if unemployed, could begin to relax. Cocktails consisted of better booze than most of the crew had ever had at home, and martinis were a favorite, served in water glasses filled to the brim.

A frequent visitor to The Swamp parties was the Catholic chaplain of the area, Father John Patrick Mulcahy, a native of San Diego and former Maryknoll missionary. He was lean, hungry-looking, hook-nosed, red-haired, and, in the eyes of the Swampmen, one of a kind.

The occupants of The Swamp had loose religious affiliations. Hawkeye claimed he had been brought up to be an all-over Baptist but that he had lost his nerve at the last minute. Duke was a foot-washing Baptist, and Trapper John was a former mackerel-snapper who had turned in his knee pads. It was the Duke who hung the name of Dago Red on the Father, and the Father accepted it with good humor.

Prior to being in the Army, Dago Red had spent five years in China and seven years on the top of a mountain in Bolivia. His contacts had been limited. With Duke and Hawkeye and Trapper John he found stimulation in conversation that included politics, surgery, sin, baseball, literature and religion. Dago Red combined the dignity of his profession and the wisdom, understanding and compassion of an honest missionary with the ability to tolerate the Swampmen. He became one of them.

At two o'clock one morning, Hawkeye and Trapper John were fighting what seemed to be a losing battle in the OR with a kid who had been shot through both chest and belly. Despite control of hemorrhage and administration of blood, the patient, whose peritoneum had been contaminated for ten hours by spillage from his lacerated colon, went deeper and deeper into shock.

"Maybe we'd better get Dago Red," said Hawkeye.

"Call Dago," ordered Trapper John.

A corpsman went for him. Within minutes he appeared.

"What can I do for you fellows?" asked the Father.

"Put in a fix," said Hawkeye. "This kid looks like a loser."

Father Mulcahy administered the last rites. Shortly thereafter, the patient's blood pressure rose from nowhere to 100, his pulse slowed to 90, and he went on to recover.

From then on Dago Red put in many a fix. With the Swampmen it was mostly a gag, but one they could not quite bring themselves to forgo when things were rough. As far as Red was concerned, of course, it was no joke. He spent many sleepless nights applying fixes and feeding beer, whiskey, coffee or consolation to distraught surgeons whose patients had not responded to the fix or who were waiting for the fix to take.

This was all to the good, except that Duke Forrest became somewhat bothered. Protestantism was strong in him, and close association with an accredited representative of the opposition caused occasional qualms.

"Y'all seem to be a mighty effective bead-jiggler, Dago," he said one night, "but how do I know one of my boys couldn't do as well?"

"I'm sure he could," Red answered calmly.

"Tell y'all what I'm gonna do," Duke said. "I'm gonna get Shaking Sammy to put in a fix the next time I need one."

Shaking Sammy was the Protestant chaplain. His headquarters were in an engineering outfit down the road. He was called Shaking Sammy because he so dearly loved to shake hands. Whenever he hit the hospital, Shaking Sammy started shaking hands as soon as he came in and kept right on shaking. On one great morning, people whose hands were shaken by Sammy as soon as he entered the compound maneuvered into his path again and again as he made his rounds and shook his eager hand again and again. It took Sammy two hours to make the circle, and he had shaken hands three hundred times with fifty people.

Despite repeated warnings, Shaking Sammy also had the bad habit of writing letters home for wounded soldiers without inquiring into the nature of their wounds. One day, before Duke had a chance to invite him in for a fix, Sammy wrote a letter for a boy who died two hours later. The letter told his mother that all was well and that he'd be home soon. It had been written with no investigation of his surgical situation. The nurse had managed to see the letter, and she told Duke and Hawkeye. They escorted Shaking Sammy out of the hospital and, as he left, they shot all four tires of his jeep with their .45's. That was the last of Shaking Sammy for a while.

"Guess I'll have to stick with the bead-jiggler," said the Duke that afternoon. "Do you suppose we could convert him?"

Discussion of conversion was cut short by the arrival of a chopper with two seriously wounded soldiers. One of them, it seemed clear from the wound of entrance, the distended abdomen, and the severe degree of shock, had a hole in his inferior vena cava or possibly in the abdominal aorta. Since the inferior vena cava and the abdominal aorta drain blood

38

from and supply blood to the lower half of the body, he was not long for this world.

Hawkeye, Duke and Trapper John went to work. They got blood going, and they gave him Levophed to raise his blood pressure. Ordinarily they would have waited for things to stabilize, but now there was no time.

Ugly John Black, the anesthesiologist, placed the tube in the trachea, through which he gave and controlled the anesthesia. Hawkeye Pierce was at the knife, and in they went. They tied off the vena cava faster than would have been considered proper in civilian surgery. Hawkeye jammed a large bore needle into the aorta so that they could pump blood through the real main line.

"Get Dago Red quick," yelled Hawkeye at the first lull.

Father Mulcahy was already entering the OR.

"What will it be, boys?" he said.

"All the Cross Action you got, plain or fancy, but make it good," said Hawkeye.

With continued blood replacement and with Levophed, hope began to emerge from what had been desperation and chaos. The patient's youth and vigor, plus rapid surgery and the remarkably effective Cross Action from Dago Red, added up to a virtual miracle.

Duke and Hawkeye were off duty the following Saturday night, and they had, perhaps, a few more than were necessary.

"We got to do something for Dago Red," said Duke. "I mean to show our appreciation for all the good fixes, bead jiggling, and skillful Cross Action."

"There's no doubt about it," replied Hawkeye. "Did you have anything in mind?"

"Ain't nothing jelled exactly, but it's gotta be something impressive."

"How about a human sacrifice?"

39

"Hawkeye," said the Duke, "y'all are purely a genius. Let's get Shaking Sammy."

"A wise choice," replied the Hawk. "You get a jeep, and I'll round up Trapper John."

Within minutes they were streaking through the darkness down the road toward the engineer outfit where Shaking Sammy made his home. Sammy was taken in his sleep, bound, gagged and tossed into the back of the jeep.

At six o'clock on Sunday morning, as Dago Red appeared at the chaplain's tent to conduct early Mass, a frightening sight confronted him. He saw a cross. Lashed to it was his Protestant colleague, Shaking Sammy. Surrounding him on the ground was a pile of hay, assorted flammable junk and a couple of old mattresses. Lying on the mattresses were Captains Pierce, Forrest, and McIntyre.

"What's going on here?" asked Father John Patrick Mulcahy.

"It's something we gotta do," answered Trapper John.

"You guys are drunk!" the Father bellowed.

"We had a drink or two," the Duke said.

"Break this up before you get in trouble," the Father said, and then he saw the fifth in Duke's hand. "Give me that bottle, Duke."

"This ain't no bottle, Red," said Duke, showing him the rag stuffed in the neck of the bottle. "I'm chairman of the Fiery Cross Committee, and this here's a Molotov cocktail."

"This is in your honor, Red," said Hawkeye. "Step back and enjoy it. The time has come."

He lifted a gasoline can and poured the contents on the debris surrounding Shaking Sammy and some on Sammy himself. By now a crowd had gathered, sleepy, perplexed, but beginning to take interest.

"Dr. John Francis Xavier McIntyre will say grace," announced Hawkeye Pierce, "or whatever the hell you call it."

40

"I don't care if it rains or freezes," intoned Trapper John, "Sammy'll be safe in the arms of Jesus."

Although several people lunged at the Duke, he lit the wick of the Molotov cocktail and hurled it into Shaking Sammy's funeral pyre. Sammy screamed, and the Swampmen took off for The Swamp. As the crowd surged forward the Molotov sizzled and went out.

Pouring three shots, Hawkeye said, "You know, the silly bastard really thought it was gasoline we poured on him. After that letter and God only knows how many others he's written, I'm kinda sorry it wasn't."

"This is going to mean trouble," said Trapper John. "Nobody will put up with that kind of crap."

"Not ordinarily," said Hawkeye, "but we'll get away with it."

"Why?" asked Duke.

"Because at seven o'clock tonight three companies of Canadians are going for Hill 55. When they do, this place will be flooded with casualties. Personally, I don't plan to work if I'm under arrest."

"Who says?" said Trapper.

"The Canadian colonel told me last night."

"Well, we'll see," said Trapper. "Barricade that door, and let's go to bed."

When they awakened at four o'clock in the afternoon, all was quiet. Duke peeked out the door and closed it quickly.

"What do the initials M.P. stand for?" he inquired.

"Shore Patrol," answered Trapper John.

Hawkeye peeked through the rear of the tent and saw that the back was unguarded. He washed, combed his hair, put on clean clothes, a hat, captain's bars and all the appurtenances of military costume he had hardly ever worn. He went under the rear tent flap, and his tentmates quickly tied things back in place. A few moments later, a smiling Captain

41

Pierce approached the two M.P.'s and returned their salutes.

"Colonel Blake says you can go back to your outfit, boys," he told them. "It's all blown over. You'd better get going before it's too dark."

The day was cold, and they took off gratefully. An hour later, after one leisurely martini apiece, the men of The Swamp strolled into the mess hall and sat down. The Colonel stared at them, spluttered, and pounded his fist on the table.

"Where are those M.P.'s?" he screamed. "You guys are confined to your tent until they come for you from Seoul."

"Y'all mean the Shore Patrol?" asked Duke innocently.

Henry shook. His mouth moved but no words came.

"What M.P.'s, Henry?" inquired Hawkeye. "Somebody screw up? We been in bed all day. Bring us up to date."

"Grab them!" yelled Henry, forgetting in his frenzy that no one else was present at the moment except nurses.

Nobody moved.

"Y'all heard your Cuhnnel," said Duke to the nurses. "Grab us."

"I'll try anything once," said Trapper John.

"I'm hornier than a three-balled tom cat," agreed Hawkeye. "Clear the tables for action."

At this point Dago Red walked in.

"Come with me," he ordered, pushing and shoving them out of the mess hall and herding them back to The Swamp. There, disillusioned and disappointed, he scolded, pleaded and insisted that they apologize to Shaking Sammy.

"Red," said Hawkeye, "I'm perfectly serious now. I'm not going to apologize to Shaking Sammy. I despise quack doctors, and for the same good reasons I despise quack sky pilots and all the screwballs on the fringe of the do-gooding business. So forget it."

Before the discussion got any further, the rumor of Canadians attacking 55 was borne out. Ambulances and helicopters disgorged dozens of wounded. The Swampmen forgot the problems arising from human sacrificial ceremonies and went to the OR. To no one's surprise, no one tried to stop them. For the next four days they worked with little letup, and no mention was made of the sacrificial ceremony of the previous Sunday.

After five days the worst was over, the preop ward was cleaned out, and no new casualties were coming. The Swampmen had a drink at nine-thirty on a bright warm morning and put on their cleanest clothes. They borrowed handcuffs from the supply sergeant. They got three of their enlisted men friends to cuff them together and guard them with rifles. They sat huddled on the ground in front of Colonel Blake's tent, passed a bottle back and forth, and chanted their version of "The Prisoner's Song."

> If we had the wings of a Colonel,
> We'd fly to the high Pyrenees,
> And open an open air laundry,
> Specializing in Blake's B.V.D.'s.

Colonel Blake came out to see what was going on.

"Hey, Henry!" yelled Hawkeye. "Can officers get broads into Leavenworth?"

In times of stress Colonel Blake sometimes stuttered.

"You c-c-crazy bastards, get the h-h-hell out of here. They don't have any replacements for you, but if you don't get out of my sight so h-h-help me C-C-Christ I'll have you s-s-shot."

5 Captain Walter Koskiusko Waldowski, of Hamtramck, Michigan, and Dental Officer of the 4077th MASH, was a very good dentist. He took care of the tusks of hundreds of troops, most of whom, before they met him, would have preferred to storm a gook bunker barehanded rather than go to a dentist. He wired fractured jaws and extracted teeth with a dexterity that few of the medical personnel had ever witnessed at home. That he should be called The Painless Pole was so obvious that no one would own up to being the originator of the nickname.

The Painless Pole ran the only truly popular Dental Clinic in the Far East Command, or at least in Korea. This clinic had a real poker table. It had a small portable pool table, a record player, a large supply of beer and other potables, and also one dental chair. At times of maximum surgical-military stress there were short intervals when the perpetual poker game might cease for a few brief hours. This was rare, however, for even when work was most intense, the poker game would often be the same. The players might change every

44

fifteen minutes, but there were always players. Some were trying to relax enough to sleep. Some were trying to wake up. At any given time, a few of the players were likely to be patients. Perhaps they were waiting for Painless to get out of the OR; perhaps they were bleeding from an extraction and passing the time until the hemorrhage was definitely controlled. Other participants were wanderers from here and there who knew they could always find a game at the Painless Polish Poker and Dental Clinic.

As a consequence, Captain Waldowski was widely known in the area and the most popular man in the outfit. Unlike most of the medical officers, he had been in private practice prior to being drafted. Unlike most of the medical officers, he had actually made a living, a state of grace almost inconceivable to his associates. He liked everyone, and was seldom without company.

His greatest hobby and interest, however, aside from managing the Poker and Dental Clinic, was women. As he was unmarried, it would have been perfectly natural for him to play the local nurses and patronize the flesh emporia in Seoul, but he passed these up much as a major league ballplayer would pass up a sandlot baseball game. Back home in Hamtramck, his reminiscences made clear, he had the highest lifetime batting average in the history of the league. At the present time he was engaged to, as best he could remember, three young lovelies, and while this sort of talk is so common in any military organization that it is automatically written off as malarkey, in his case it could not be written off, even by the most skeptical.

The Painless Pole, beyond any shadow of a doubt, was the best-equipped dentist in the U.S. Army Dental Corps. He was the owner and operator of the Pride of Hamtramck. Officers and enlisted men from the entire area frequently visited the 4077th MASH, supposedly to take advantage of the shower facilities, but actually they came in hope of catching a glimpse. In fact, Dr. Waldowski's dental assistant, a Corporal Jones, significantly enhanced his lowly wages by informing certain troops in advance of the Captain's intention of bathing. In the shower, popeyed officers and enlisted men viewed the Pride wistfully, and one day a corporal from Mississippi spoke for them all.

"Ah'd purely love," he said, "to see it angry."

Unfortunately, about once a month, the Painless Pole underwent a period of depression lasting no less than twenty-four hours and seldom more than three days. The usual activities of the Clinic continued, but except when forced to work, Walt just lay in his sack and stared at the walls. Radar O'Reilly, of course, was able to predict the advent of these episodes several days in advance, so that the clients of the Clinic were forewarned, but it was Hawkeye Pierce who spread the first word of what turned out to be Captain Waldowski's most serious seizure.

On this afternoon Hawkeye had been working continuously for twelve hours and, having finally finished and found it to be bathing time, he had gone to the shower tent. He undressed slowly. His stethoscope fell out of the rear pocket of his fatigue pants, and he hung it on a nail along with the pants. He stepped under the shower, luxuriated in its warmth, relaxed and dreamed dreams of Crabapple Cove. Returning to reality, he walked back to the bench where he had left his clothes. He found Captain Walter Waldowski, The Painless Pole, sitting on the bench. All the Dental Officer had on was Hawkeye's stethoscope and a look of great alarm. He was listening to the Pride of Hamtramck.

"What's the matter, Walt?" asked Hawkeye.

"I think it's dead," Walt answered and, in a trance, he walked to the nearest shower with the stethoscope still dangling from his ears.

That evening The Painless Pole entered The Swamp and

sat down. He was given a drink, which he accepted with indifference.

"I thought you guys oughta know," he announced.

"Know what?"

"I'm going to commit suicide."

There was a moment of silence. Finally Trapper John leaned from his sack and grasped Walt's hand.

"We'll miss you, Walt," he said. "I hope you'll be happy in your new location."

"Hey, Walt, how about you all leaving me your record player?" requested Duke.

"When are you making the trip?" inquired Hawkeye. "You oughta give Henry a little warning so he can get a replacement."

Throughout the interrogation, The Painless Pole sat numbly and made no effort to answer.

"How do you figure to go?" continued Trapper. "You gonna do the .45 between the eyes, or are you planning something a little more refined?"

"That's what I wanted to ask," Walt finally said. "What would you guys recommend?"

"The forty-five will do it," Duke answered. "There's no question about that, but it can be sloppy. How about the black capsule?"

"What's that?"

"It's a never miss, easy, pleasant ride," explained Hawkeye. "You have a few drinks, take the black capsule, and the next thing you know you're listening to the heavenly chorus singing the Hamtramck High School victory song."

"You guys got any black capsules?"

"For a buddy like y'all," the Duke told him, "we'll sure as hell get some, if that's what you want."

"That's what I want. I gotta go make out my will. Duke, you can have the record player. I'm closing the Clinic in the morning. Tomorrow night is it. You guys come up. We'll have a few drinks, and I'll take a black capsule, or maybe two."

The Painless Pole left. Hawkeye followed him.

"Relieve me in three hours," he instructed the Swampmen as he departed. "We'd better watch the foolish bastard until he gets over this one."

The next morning Henry heard about it. He was all upset and making plans to evacuate Painless, and came to The Swamp to discuss it.

"What in hell's wrong with him anyhow? Why do I have to get saddled with all the screwballs in the whole U.S. Army? Where in hell am I going to get another dentist?"

Trapper was in the Dental Clinic doing guard duty, but Duke and Hawkeye argued Henry out of his evacuation plans.

"Y'all don't need to get rid of him, Henry," said Duke. "He'll get the hell over it."

"Christ, Henry," Hawk added, "if you get rid of him, some head-shrinker will just give him shock treatments and probably send him to another outfit. We can give him some shock treatments right here!"

"I'm afraid not, boys," Henry said. "This sort of thing is dynamite. If he pushed himself over up here, I'd never hear the end of it."

"Henry, you surely are aware," Hawkeye continued, "of the immense prestige which the presence of the Pride bestows upon the unit. Furthermore, the Pride is the greatest drawing card any military shower tent ever had. You must realize that the personnel of our hospital and all nearby troops, in their zeal to view the Pride of Hamtramck, have become the cleanest goddam soldiers in Korea. Henry, in the name of sanitation and personal hygiene, will you just give us twenty-four hours to cure Painless Waldowski?"

"Yeah, Henry," Duke said. "Will y'all just do that?"

"I'm crazy. I'm just as crazy as you guys. Go ahead, cure him, and let me the hell out of here!" he cried, leaving.

"So," Hawkeye said to the Duke, "how are we going to cure him?"

"Easy," the Duke said. "We'll get some kind of black capsule, like we told him, stick about fifteen grains of amytal in it, get him loaded, and give him the capsule. By the time he wakes up, he oughta be O.K."

"We better have some benzedrine or something around in case he looks like he won't wake up."

"Yeah, I guess so."

"We should fancy up the procedure a little, too. We can work that out today. Let's start by lining up Dago Red."

They ambled over to the chaplain's tent, entered and opened two of Father Mulcahy's beers.

"How they goin', Losing Preacher?" asked Hawkeye. "Whadda you hear from the Pope?"

"What do you reprobates want?"

"We came to invite y'all to the Last Supper," explained the Duke.

"The Painless Pole," Hawkeye explained, "plans to cross the Great Divide about eleven tonight and wishes his friends and cronies to break bread and wine with him beforehand. He has also requested that Losing Preacher Mulcahy come prepared to administer the last rites of the bead-jiggler Church. He has been somewhat slack in his devotion to the Church in recent years and wishes you to grease the skids a little."

"Why don't you guys leave me alone? What's this all about anyway?" Dago asked wearily.

"We're serious, Red," Hawkeye said. "Painless has parted his mooring. We don't want to have him evacuated because he's a good guy and we like him and we figure we need him. We think we can get him straightened out, but we need a little help."

"What do you want me to do?"

"Just what we said. Come up, have supper, a few drinks, put in one of your well-known fixes, and don't get annoyed at anything you hear or see."

"OK, boys, I'll trust you," Father Mulcahy agreed, "but I hope the big guy in Rome never gets wind of it."

"He sure as hell won't hear it from me," Hawkeye assured him.

They went to the supply sergeant and commissioned the construction of a coffin.

"Who you planning to kill?" the sergeant asked.

"Nobody. We need the coffin for Painless. He is going to commit suicide."

"He can't do that!" protested the sergeant.

"Why can't he?"

"Dentists we got lots of, but there's only one Pride of Hamtramck."

"So what?"

"So what? It belongs to the world! You gotta stop him."

"Don't worry, we're not gonna let him do it. You seen Radar O'Reilly around?"

"Radar went to Seoul to get some blood. He'll be back this afternoon. Whadda you want with him?"

"We may need him. Send him over to The Swamp as soon as he gets back."

In the pharmacy a black capsule was prepared. Then the two trooped over to the mess hall and found the celebrated chef, Sergeant Mother Divine. Sergeant Mother Divine was a Negro boy from Brooklyn who, during his military career, had distinguished himself through a variety of accomplishments, not all of them culinary. As president of the Brooklyn and Manhattan Marked-Down Monument and Landmark Company, and equipped with picture postcards and impressive papers suggesting ownership of various public edifices, statuary and parks, he had, for months, been running a thriving sales business. Just two days before the visit of Hawkeye and Duke, in fact, he had sold the Brooklyn Botanical Garden for two hundred dollars to a Caucasian private from Mississippi.

"Man," one of his less sophisticated kitchen colleagues had said to him, more in awe than admonition, "how could you do that?"

"Man," Mother Divine said, "it was easy. That cat wouldn't buy the bridge because he said he'd heard in the family for years that his grandpappy had bought it a long time ago."

"Mother," Hawkeye said to him now, "how would you like to win the Medaille d'Honneur des Chevaliers d'Escoffier de France?"

"Man," Mother said, "what is it?"

"It's a gold medal," Hawkeye said.

"Man," Mother said.

"It's awarded in Paris every year," Hawkeye said, "to the man voted the Chef of the Year."

"And how do I get voted to that?" Mother asked.

"By preparing for this evening an especially sumptuous . . ."

"Oh no, man," Mother said. "I ain't caterin' to no special parties. That ain't in the regulations. In the regulations I just gotta provide three . . ."

"Mother," Hawkeye said, "you like Captain Waldowski, don't you?"

"That's right," Mother said. "In fact, there's somethin' about that man I greatly admire."

With that as his cue, and with the Duke nodding assent, Hawkeye launched into an explanation of the emotional and mental state of the Painless Pole and then an impassioned plea. When he finished, Mother Divine agreed to do his part to save the Pride of Hamtramck.

In the Clinic that evening the poker game was stopped, and the poker and pool facilities, along with the dental chair, were removed. Two long tables were transported from the mess hall, candles were lighted and the Swampmen tended bar. The guests—doctors, chopper pilots, enlisted men— began to warm up, but Painless Waldowski sat unhappily in a corner, barely acknowledging the greetings of his friends and admirers.

At the stroke of midnight the Last Supper was served, and no finer meal had ever been prepared at the 4077th MASH. This was due not only to the inspired efforts of Mother Divine but also to the fact that a Canadian supply truck had been hijacked a few miles to the south that very afternoon. As a result, smoked Gaspé salmon was followed by Pea Soup Habitant, roast beef sliced to the individual's preference, three vegetables, tossed salad, baked alaska, coffee or tea, Drambuie and Antonio y Cleopatra cigars.

Painless drank reluctantly and little, but Duke saw to it that the drinks were high in alcoholic content. Painless ate without appetite and at the conclusion of the meal, as each guest rose to make a short speech of fondness and farewell, he barely acknowledged the tributes and good wishes.

When the speeches had been completed, the coffin was carried in. It was lined with blankets and supplied with three fresh decks of cards, a box of poker chips, a fifth of Scotch, several basic dental instruments and pictures of Painless Waldowski's three fiancées. For the first time Painless showed some interest.

"What's that?" he asked.

"The coffin for y'all," the Duke informed him.

"But I'm not even dead yet."

"Yeah, but you're a pretty big guy," Hawkeye said. "We don't want to have to lug you around after you take the black capsule. We figured you could get in the box and then take it. Really, Painless, it'll be a helluva lot more convenient."

Painless looked doubtful.

"Hey, Painless," someone else asked, "which way do you think you'll go? Up or down?"

"I've asked the Father to arrange that," he said, glancing at Dago Red.

"You sure you still got an inside track, Red?" asked Trapper John. "If there's any chance of a slip-up, Painless might change his mind."

"My mind's made up," asserted the Painless Pole.

Father Mulcahy administered the last rites. As he concluded, there was a murmur of approval. This had been one of Red's best and most elaborate fixes.

"Well stroked," said the Duke.

As Painless prepared to enter the coffin and take the black capsule, Trapper and Hawkeye were watching the door anxiously. Suddenly it was thrown open and Radar O'Reilly burst in upon the gathering and, gasping for breath, yelled, "Hold everything!"

"What's the matter?" Hawkeye said.

"I just got the message," Radar said. "Painless needs a parachute. The fix didn't take, and he goes down."

A low, sudden rumble of discontent swept the room. The group turned its attention to Father Mulcahy.

"What's wrong, Red?" demanded Trapper John. "You lose your stuff?"

"Never mind the recriminations," said Hawkeye. "Let's get on with it."

He produced a parachute, and one of the chopper pilots helped him get Painless Waldowski into it. By now Painless was feeling the booze.

"I don't want to be a parachute jumper," he complained. "I might get killed."

"You just might," Hawkeye consoled him. "Get in here, Painless. It's time for take-off."

Complete with parachute, Painless got into the coffin. He

took the black capsule and washed it down with a shot of Scotch. Within five minutes, he was in dreamland.

Trapper John came forward with a blue ribbon. Reverently, but loosely, he tied it around the Pride of Hamtramck, and the poker game started. At frequent intervals, one or another of the Swampmen got up to check their dentist's pulse, respiration and blood pressure.

On one occasion, when Painless seemed a little deeper than desirable, he was given a small dose of stimulant. By daybreak, he showed signs of recovery. He was removed from the coffin and taken to a waiting helicopter of the 5th Air Rescue Squadron parked just behind the preop ward. At a height of about fifty feet over the ballfield, directly in front of The Swamp, he was given a large shot of benzedrine intravenously and lowered from the chopper by a rope. A string attached to the ripcord was pulled, and the chute opened. A rescue crew waited below holding a blanket. The pilot released the rope. Painless and his parachute, to the cheers of the gathering, plummeted eight feet into the blanket.

While the chute was being removed, Painless rubbed his eyes, looked around and said, "What the hell's going on, boys?"

"That's what we'd like to know," said Hawkeye. "Come into The Swamp."

"You look dry," said Trapper, handing him a can of beer. "Where you've been, I hear you can get a thirst. Tell us about it. How'd you get back?"

"I'll be with you in a minute," said Captain Waldowski, leaving the tent after downing the beer in three gulps.

Upon his return, Painless, obviously proud and holding a blue ribbon in his hand, informed them, "I don't know where I've been, but wherever it was I sure as hell won first prize. How about a game of poker?"

6

The other doctors in the 4077th spent a great deal of time in discussion of the men of The Swamp. When Duke's name was mentioned, it was generally agreed that he was the most amiable, and therefore likeable, of the three. Trapper John's consummate skill as a surgeon earned him the most respect, but when it came to Hawkeye Pierce there was a great divergence of opinion.

The man who hated Hawkeye the most was Captain Frank Burns. He had good reason. He was persecuted by Hawkeye Pierce. Captain Burns was the boss of one surgical shift, and Hawkeye of the other. Working times frequently overlapped, so some contact was inevitable. The more contact they had, the more they hated each other.

Frank Burns was the son of a general practitioner and surgeon in a medium-sized Indiana town. After one year of internship, and as heir apparent, he had joined his father in practice for three years before being drafted. He owned a thirty-five-thousand-dollar house and two automobiles.

Hawkeye Pierce had spent the same three years in a surgical residency, without salary, and had been supported by his wife and hospital poker games. In Hawkeye's opinion, Frank Burns, despite a definite technical competency, seldom thought and was a fake. In Frank Burns's opinion, Hawkeye Pierce was an uncouth yokel who failed to understand that learning surgery from a father who didn't know any was better than formal training in a teaching hospital.

Captain Burns, born to affluence, accustomed to authority, was very definitely the boss of his shift. He found the enlisted men exasperating. At least once a week, it was necessary for him to report someone to Colonel Blake for dereliction of duty. It then became necessary for Captain Pierce to intercede in behalf of the enlisted man, which he always did successfully. This annoyed Captain Burns, and one day he approached Captain Pierce and attempted to discuss the subject.

"Frank," Hawkeye said, "you stink. I haven't decided what to do about you, but sooner or later I'll come to some sort of decision. Now I suggest that you go to bed and lull yourself to sleep counting your annuities or something, before you precipitate my decision, to the sorrow of us both."

Frank ran to Colonel Blake and complained. Colonel Blake came to The Swamp.

"Pierce," he asked, "what ails you?"

"Well," said Hawkeye, "the guy from the Sox who looked me over once said that, in addition to having a very weak throwing arm, I'd never hit big-league pitching."

"Jesus," said Henry, "you *are* crazy. Anyhow, you leave Burns alone. I know what you mean about him, but surgeons of any kind are hard to find. Leave him alone, or it's gonna be your ass."

"Yes, my leader," agreed Hawkeye meekly, as Henry stormed out.

That night when Hawkeye went to work he encountered Frank.

"Hey, Frank," he said, "one of my kid brothers just got out of jail. I wrote him and told him to go out to Indiana and burn down your thirty-five-thousand-dollar-house."

Again, Frank ran to Colonel Blake who visited Hawkeye in the morning.

"Pierce, have you flipped?" he demanded.

"Whadda ya mean?" asked Hawkeye, who had forgotten all about it.

"I heard what you said to Frank last night about your brother burning his house down."

"Which brother? I got six."

"The one who just got out of jail."

"Well, for Chrissake, Henry, I can't keep track of things from here. It could be any of them. They all sort of rotate in and out. Forget it. None of them could find Indiana on the best day he ever had."

When Hawkeye, for the moment and to placate Colonel Blake, let up on Captain Burns, it was Duke Forrest who took over, again in behalf of the enlisted men. This time it was in behalf of Private Lorenzo Boone, the dunce of the Double Natural.

In his nineteen years, Private Boone had been exposed to very little, so his real abilities were difficult to assess. He couldn't seem to do anything right, which may have been why the Army assigned him to a Mobile Army Surgical Hospital, where he was given the job of third assistant bedpan jockey in the postop ward. Inept though he was, he did try hard, and he improved with time.

For a while Private Boone was assigned the simple job of computing the liquid intake and output of the more severely ill patients. This was really quite easy. Most of the patients received only intravenous fluids for intake, and they all had catheters in their bladders, so there was no problem in measuring the urinary output. In accordance with medical custom, Private Boone was supposed to measure these quantities in cubic centimeters (cc's), of which there are one thousand to a quart.

After a few days, the intake figures recorded by Private Boone became open to question. Several patients were alleged to have taken only one cc, two cc's, or in extreme cases four or five cc's in a given twenty-four-hour period, and no output at all was recorded. The ensuing revelation that Private Boone thought cc's stood for cups of coffee solved part of the problem but did little to increase his efficiency.

It was shortly after this that Captain Burns was taken ill. In fact, he was so indisposed that he spent three days in his tent and, although the nature of his illness was never widely known, its origins were as follows:

Captain Burns was addicted to a common failing in the surgical dodge: if a patient died, he claimed it was (1) God's will or (2) someone else's fault. One day he spent six long, hard hours operating on a severely wounded soldier, who'd been in deep shock throughout most of the procedure. Half an hour after surgery, the patient died in the postoperative ward. His final gesture was to vomit and aspirate some of the vomitus. Private Boone, on his own initiative, quickly brought in a suction machine.

It was not functioning, but neither was the patient as Captain Burns appeared and observed Private Boone's futile efforts.

"Boone," he said, "you killed my patient!"

Private Boone turned white. He walked away and went to a dark corner and cried. The Captain said he'd killed a man, and the Captain was a doctor and he ought to know.

Duke Forrest caught it. To Captain Burns he said, "Frank, may I speak to y'all outside for a moment?"

Korean nights can be dark. Often you can't see your hand in front of your face. Captain Burns never saw the hand that broke his nose, split his lip, or the knee that made him terribly uncomfortable for three days to come.

Trapper John was next in line to take on Captain Burns, and it had to do with cardiac massage. Cardiac massage is manual compression of a heart that has stopped. It is done through a hole hastily made in the chest in the hope, usually forlorn, that the heartbeat will resume and the patient will recover. The administrator of cardiac massage compresses and releases the heart between the fingers of one hand with a rhythm designed to approximate the normal heartbeat, and Captain Frank Burns was, without doubt, the leading cardiac masseur in the Far East Command.

At breakfast one morning Trapper John McIntyre, leaving the mess hall, encountered Captain Frank Burns entering the mess hall. Trapper John traveled a fast right to Frank's jaw, and Frank dropped on the sand floor like a poleaxed steer.

This was the second time within a month that Frank had been assaulted by a Swampman. The first time had been clandestine, but this was public, and again an irate Henry entered The Swamp.

Standing over Trapper John, who was sipping a beer in his sleeping bag, Colonel Blake yelled his usual question. "What's wrong with you, anyhow?"

"I'm wondering the same thing, Henry," replied Trapper. "I hear the son-of-a-bitch got up. I guess I've lost my punch."

Trapper rolled over and ignored Henry.

"You wanta know what it's all about, Henry?" volunteered Hawkeye.

"Yeah, I sure do!"

"Well, you remember, yesterday morning was pretty busy. The most minor injury was a kid with a shell-fragment wound in his right thigh. It didn't look like much. Frank decided to get him out of the way so they could get on with the others. As usual, he didn't think. He took the kid in with a pressure of eighty over fifty, had them give him anesthesia, and started to debride the wound. It turned out the kid's femoral artery was lacerated and he bled a lot. Then he had a cardiac arrest, and Frank rubbed his heart. It came back, he stopped the bleeding and got some blood into him, and by midafternoon he looked OK. By the time we came on duty last night the kid was in shock again. Trapper took over, figured he was bleeding from the chest wound Frank made, got his pressure up, and opened his chest again to stop the bleeding.

"Now the kid's OK," Hawkeye said, "but because that bastard Burns didn't observe a few basic principles, the boy almost died. Instead of cussing himself out for almost losing a patient, Frank thinks he's a big hero because he did a successful cardiac massage. Therefore Trapper John administered a knuckle sandwich."

It took a femme fatale, however, to restore peace, more or less, to the 4077th MASH. She was Major Margaret Houlihan, new Chief Nurse, and one June morning she emerged, not out of a scallop shell like Botticelli's Venus, but out of a helicopter. She was tallish, willowish, blondish, fortyish. She had a nice figure. In fact, she was a nice-looking, forty-year-old female.

Within the prescribed twenty-four hours following her arrival, Major Houlihan made a point of seeking out the boss of each shift and attempting to discuss nursing problems with him. Captain Burns was in starched fatigues and his most gracious mood, but he mentioned several nurses whose performance was inadequate and made a variety of suggestions for improvement. The Major was quite impressed with Captain Burns.

She was less impressed with Captain Pierce. She found him in the mess tent in soiled fatigues having a late breakfast. She introduced herself, and Hawkeye invited her to join him over a cup of coffee.

"Captain Pierce," Major Houlihan said, "I observed the night shift and I was not at all impressed with some of our nurses. How do you feel, Captain, about the nursing situation here?"

"Major," Hawkeye said, "this is a team effort. I'm responsible for my team. It consists of doctors, nurses and enlisted men. We've been working as a unit for six months with little change in personnel. I'm satisfied with them."

"Well," she said, "Captain Burns isn't at all satisfied."

"Mother," said Hawkeye Pierce, "Captain Burns is a jerk, and if you don't know it by now you . . ."

Major Houlihan arose. "I wonder," she asked, "how anyone like you reaches such a position of responsibility in the Army Medical Corps."

"Honey," answered Hawkeye, "if I knew the answer to that I sure as hell wouldn't be here."

"Very well, Captain," Major Houlihan said. "It appears that we are not going to get along. Nevertheless, I want you to know that I will attempt to cooperate with you in every possible way."

"Major," Hawkeye said, smiling, "I appreciate that, so would you consider another cup of coffee?"

Reluctantly she sat down again and resumed the talk. She was still terribly upset, so Hawkeye tried to explain a few things.

"Major," he said, "you're watching both shifts. Watch them with an eye to which shift does the most work with the least fuss. Watch them with an eye to how many people work happily or unhappily."

"I observed last night that both nurses and enlisted men addressed you as 'Hawkeye'."

"That's my name."

"Such familiarity is highly improper," declaimed Major Houlihan, "and inconsistent with maximum efficiency in an organization such as this."

"Well, Major," said Hawkeye as he got up and left, "I'm gonna have a couple shots of Scotch and go to bed. Obviously you're a female version of the routine Regular Army Clown. Stay away from me and my gang, and we'll get along fine. See you around the campus."

Having been summarily dismissed by Captain Pierce, Major Houlihan took her problems to the commanding officer. The interview was quite unsatisfactory. Colonel Blake told her, after she'd bothered him enough, that he'd rather get rid of Captain Burns than Captain Pierce, but couldn't afford to lose either one.

Major Houlihan was quite upset, but withheld final judgment for a week. By the end of that period she was completely convinced that the Swampmen, Pierce in particular, exerted an evil influence upon the Colonel and upon the whole outfit. Captain Burns, she learned from frequent observation, was a brilliant technical surgeon. His behavior was military, his dress and bearing were military. He was, she felt, an officer, a gentleman and a surgeon.

The obvious continued to escape her. For months Captain Burns's group had been getting into difficulties. Some of its members, when in doubt, bypassed Frank Burns and asked the Swampmen for help. As a result, Colonel Blake finally decided to create a Chief Surgeon, whose duty, in addition to doing his fair share of the work, would be to assist each shift in the management of the most difficult cases. Everyone in the organization except Captain Burns and Major Houlihan recognized that this job could logically be given only to Trapper John, and so it was.

Upon learning of the Colonel's decision, and certain that the commanding officer was bereft of his senses, Major Houlihan invited Captain Burns to her tent for a council of war. She gave Frank a drink. He explained to her the tragedy of turning the organization over to the riff-raff and, since she agreed with him, extolled her perspicacity. Then, over her signature, they composed to General Hammond in Seoul a letter that he would never receive because Hawkeye had the mail clerk censoring the Major's outgoing correspondence. After that the Major gave Frank another drink, and Frank embraced and kissed her. Then they departed, reluctantly, for the mess tent. It was supper time.

In The Swamp, meanwhile, a party in honor of the newly appointed Chief Surgeon was in progress. Attendance was high, and at five-thirty it was suggested by someone and agreed upon by all that a Chief Surgeon should be treated with more than usual respect. Trapper John went along with this and requested that he be properly crowned and transported to the mess hall by native bearers. This presented complications, as crowns are hard to come by in the Korean hinterlands, and the Korean houseboys, when asked to serve as native bearers, protested that they had not hired out as such. Instead, a bedpan was fastened to Trapper John's head with adhesive tape, and Hawkeye, Duke, Ugly John and the Painless Pole picked up the sack upon which the newly crowned Chief Surgeon rested and, with the others following, bore it and him to the mess hall.

"Now y'all hear this!" the Duke announced to the assembled diners. "This here is your new Chief Surgeon. He has just been crowned, so y'all do him honor."

Then the members of the Chief Surgeon's court broke into song:

> "Hail to the Chief,
> And King of all the surgeons.
> He needs a Queen,
> To satisfy his urgins."

"That's right," Trapper John, still reclining on his sack, said. "And who's that over there?"

He pointed toward the back of the mess hall. There, sitting apart from the others and evidencing complete disgust, were Major Houlihan and Captain Burns.

63

"Oh them, Your Highness?" Hawkeye said. "That's just the goose girl and the swine herd."

"I don't like the swine herd," Trapper John said, "but I might get to like the goose girl."

Major Houlihan and Captain Burns retreated to console each other and plot their revenge. They retreated to the Major's tent, where they consoled and plotted until 1:30 A.M. At least that was the report which Corporal Radar O'Reilly submitted in the morning.

The Swampmen were at breakfast when Major Houlihan and Captain Burns entered. As the two started to pass the table, eyes front, Duke spoke up.

"Mornin', Frank," he said.

"Hiya, Hot Lips," said the Chief Surgeon to the Chief Nurse. "Now that I'm a chief, too, we really oughta get together."

Frank stopped, turned and made one menacing step toward the Swampmen.

"Join us if you wish, Frank," invited Hawkeye. "Looks like a great day to set a hen."

Captain Burns thought better of it. He escorted Major Houlihan to a distant table, but his moment came that night when he and Hawkeye found themselves together in the utility room, next to the OR, where coffee was available. Hawkeye had just poured himself a cup and was seated at the table, sipping and smoking, when Captain Burns entered and approached the coffee pot.

"Hey, Frank," said the Hawk, "is that stuff you're tappin' really any good?"

"One more word out of you," Frank erupted, screaming it, "and I'll kill you!"

"So kill me," Hawkeye said.

At that moment Colonel Henry Blake entered, and what he saw was enough to do it. He saw Captain Pierce sitting peacefully with a cup of coffee and a cigarette. He saw Captain Burns, on the other side of the room, pick up the coffee pot and hurl it at Captain Pierce, who ducked. Then he saw Captain Burns follow the coffee pot and start flailing away at Hawkeye with his fists. Hawkeye, having spotted the Colonel, did nothing but cover his head with his arms and scream.

"Henry!" he screamed. "Help me, Henry! He's gone mad!"

The next day Captain Burns was reassigned to a stateside hospital. Although the Swampmen were happy, Colonel Blake wasn't, and entered The Swamp to define his unhappiness.

"OK," he said. "You guys win another round. You ditched Frank. I could have put up with him screwing Hot Lips, if he was, which I doubt, but you guys had to have your way. I just want you to know that I know what you did. He was a jerk, I admit, but he was needed, and now we don't have him and it's your fault."

"Henry," said Hawkeye, "for Crissake, sit down and relax. Nobody needs guys like him. You're all concerned with numbers of people. The clown created more work than he accomplished. We're better off without him."

"Maybe so," Henry sighed. "I don't know."

"Henry," Duke asked, "if I get into Hot Lips and jump Hawkeye Pierce can I go home, too?"

7

Each doctors' tent at the MASH had a young Korean to clean it, keep the stove going, shine shoes, and do the laundry and other chores. He was called a houseboy.

Naturally The Swamp's houseboy was called a Swampboy. His name was Ho-Jon. Ho-Jon was tall for a Korean. He was thin. He was bright. Prior to the war he had attended a church school in Seoul. He was a Christian. His English was relatively fluent.

Ho-Jon thought Hawkeye Pierce, Duke Forrest and Trapper John McIntyre were the three greatest people in the world. Unlike other houseboys, he was allowed to spend a lot of his spare time in the tent. The Swampmen helped him with reading and writing English, had books sent to him from the States, and gave him a good basic education in a few short months. Ho-Jon had a mind like a bear trap. It engulfed everything that came its way. During bull sessions in The Swamp, he sat quietly in a corner and listened. During busy periods, he was brought to the OR and trained to assist the Swampmen as a scrub nurse.

The Swampmen thought as much of Ho-Jon as he did of them. On his seventeenth birthday, however, despite the attempt of Colonel Blake, urged on by the Swampmen, to intercede with the Korean government, Ho-Jon was drafted into the Republic of Korea Army. Unhappiness and a feeling of despair and frustration prevailed in The Swamp on the day of Ho-Jon's departure. The Swampmen gave him clothes, money, canned food, and cigarettes. Hawkeye himself drove Ho-Jon to Seoul. There the two went to see Ho-Jon's family who lived in a dirty shack on a filthy street and whose reaction to the largesse showered upon their son by the American doctors was awe-inspiring and pathetic.

Hawkeye left hastily. He found an Air Force Officer's club where he drank moodily and disinterestedly without getting any emotional benefit from the good Air Force Scotch. He never expected to see Ho-Jon again. He thought of Crabapple Cove and wondered how he could ever have thought his material benefits and opportunities limited. Compared to Ho-Jon, he'd had everything.

As it turned out, Captain Pierce did see Ho-Jon again. It was six weeks later, when Ho-Jon returned in the uniform of a private in the ROK Army. The uniform was covered with blood. Deep in Ho-Jon's chest was a mortar fragment.

At the Double Natural, as at every MASH, all wounds were first hastily assessed in the admitting ward and then the seriously wounded were brought into the preoperative ward. There blood was typed, nurses and corpsmen took blood pressures, started transfusions, inserted Foley catheters in bladders and Levin tubes in stomachs, and hung the X-rays on a wire in front of each patient's cot.

Arriving for duty on this morning and finding the preop ward full, Hawkeye, Duke and Trapper John had gone down the row of wounded and started to make their plans. When they reached the last cot a corpsman said, "This kid is pretty bad."

Hawkeye looked at the X-ray. He saw a large shell fragment deep in the boy's chest.

"This one's for you, Trapper," he said. "I'll help you, and Duke can take that belly back there."

Then Captain Pierce took his first look at the patient.

"Christ!" he said. "It's Ho-Jon."

Trapper looked.

"OK. It's Ho-Jon. We'll fix him."

Ho-Jon opened his eyes. He saw his friends and smiled.

"You'll be OK, boy," said the corpsman.

"I know," Ho-Jon whispered. "Captains Pierces and Captains McIntyres will help me."

"You know it, Ho-Jon," Captain Pierce said. "You just rest, and we'll do it after you've had one more pint of blood."

The Duke was about to become occupied in a bad belly, so they decided not to tell him. They went out for a butt.

"How do we go, Trapper?" asked Hawkeye.

"Right chest, just like the missile. He's lost some blood. I'm afraid it's hit more than just the lung. It's in deep."

"Trapper, you remember how we used to wonder what a kid like Ho-Jon might do if he had a chance to get an education?"

"Yeah," Trapper answered dully.

"If we squeeze him through, I'm going to get him into Androscoggin College."

"We'll squeeze him through and right into Dartmouth," said Trapper, grinding out his cigarette. "If all he wants to do is catch lobsters, he can learn that here."

A grim pair of surgeons went to work on Ho-Jon.

"We'll need room," said Trapper. "The sixth rib goes."

"Never mind the conversation. Do it, Dad."

They opened the pleura, put in the rib spreader, and aspirated the blood from the chest cavity. Ho-Jon's pulse and blood pressure held steady. Trapper reached down toward the inferior vena cava where it empties into the right atrium of the heart. He felt the missile.

"I got it," he said. "Here, feel."

Hawkeye felt.

"I don't feel anything."

"Oh, Jesus," moaned Trapper, and felt again.

"What happened?"

"The mother must have gone in. I can't feel it."

"I don't get it," said Hawkeye nervously.

"It must have been in the cava, and the hole sealed itself off. When I felt it I must have jiggled it just enough to turn it loose. I can't feel it in the heart. I don't feel it in the right pulmonary artery. It must be in the left pulmonary artery."

"Whadda we do?"

"Close and get an X-ray and fight another day."

"OK," Hawkeye said unhappily.

The X-ray confirmed Trapper's guess. The shell fragment was in the left pulmonary artery. Three days later Ho-Jon was out of bed, happy, proud to have been operated on by two of his three heroes and, unaware of the odds against him, not at all upset at the prospect of further surgery.

Taking a missile out of a pulmonary artery is no great trick, but few surgeons in Korea were familiar with such techniques. Cardiovascular surgery was in its infancy, and such procedures were not usually done in tents. Ordinarily this sort of case would have been evacuated to Tokyo, but no one seriously thought that any other surgeon in the Far East was better equipped to do the job than Trapper John. Colonel Blake did mention the possibility of evacuation once, but dropped the subject when Hawkeye gave him a very direct look.

In The Swamp the next week the tension grew. Humor was nonexistent. Unmilitary behavior tapered off. One evening Hawkeye passed around a bottle of Scotch, feeling that, for the sake of efficiency, they should attempt some sort of comeback.

"When do we go for it, Trapper?" he asked.

"June 2."

"Why June 2?"

"That's the day I shut out Harvard on two hits."

Trapper John did not say another word that night. He lay on his sack, sipped his drink and just looked straight up.

Ho-Jon, at the start of his big day, lay on the operating table, expectantly but confidently gazing up at Ugly John. Ugly John said, "Now, Ho-Jon, you just take it easy. Everything will be all right."

Ho-Jon smiled and said, "I know, Captains Blacks."

Ugly John started the Pentothal and curare, and three minutes later inserted the intratracheal tube through which Ho-Jon would do all his breathing while his friends worked on him. Then Ho-Jon was turned onto his right side and draped, and Trapper John, assisted by Hawkeye and Duke, removed Ho-Jon's fifth rib. With that out of the way, Trapper entered the pleural cavity, and easily located the missile wedged in the left pulmonary artery. After opening the pericardium, which surrounds the heart, he then dissected his way around the origin of the artery and placed umbilical tapes as temporary ties above and below the missile.

"How is he?" Trapper asked Ugly John.

"Nice," said Ugly. "Get on with it."

While Hawkeye applied traction on the tape above the shell fragment and Duke did the same below, Trapper incised the artery, removed the fragment, and resutured the artery with 5-0 arterial silk.

"Ease off on those tapes, and let's see how much it bleeds," said Trapper. He had to place one extra suture, and then there was no more bleeding.

"How's he doing?" Trapper asked the anesthesiologist.

"Nice," Ugly John assured him.

The Swampmen looked at one another, and Trapper said, "Boys, we're home free."

For the rest of the day relaxation ruled, and recollection of it is indistinct in the minds of the survivors, who included Ho-Jon. Soon Ho-Jon was up and around, back at his job as Swampboy, his English improving. He was losing the Korean habit of putting an "s" on the end of every word. He eagerly read all that the Swampmen provided for him.

"Now," said Hawkeye one day, "I gotta get him into Androscoggin College."

"Dartmouth," said Trapper John.

"Georgia," said Duke.

"Boys," said Hawkeye, "it's gotta be Androscoggin. Dartmouth is too big and too expensive. At Androscoggin he can start a little more slowly and get more attention. If he's as good as I think he is, he can move into the big leagues later, and, I don't think Georgia is the place even if the Klan doesn't have a chapter house there any more."

The Swampmen agreed on Androscoggin College. "Guess I'll write to the Dean," said Hawkeye and sat down to do so. He wrote:

Dr. James Lodge
Dean, Androscoggin College
Androscoggin, Maine

Dear Dr. Lodge:
    A few years having passed, perhaps you'll be willing to read a letter from me, although I seem to recall that when I left for the Army back in 1943 you indicated no great feeling of loss. The United States Army, in its infinite wisdom, allowed me to partake of the medical education for which I was so well prepared at Androscoggin.
    Now I am in Korea as a surgeon in a Mobile Army Hospital. To make a long story short, I know a Korean kid that I want to get into Androscoggin. You took a chance on

71

me. If you could do that you have twice as much reason to take a chance on my boy, Ho-Jon. He is a winner.

I'm just as serious as I can be. If you'll consider the deal at all, let me know what it will cost, and I'll see what I can do to get up the loot.

Your former outstanding undergraduate,

Hawkeye Pierce

An answer arrived three weeks later:

Dear Hawkeye:

As Dean of the College, I naturally remember you very well. In my job one has to take the bitter as well as the sweet, and I've had my share of both.

My natural expectation is that, if I accede to your request, I will soon have on my hands some illiterate seventy-year-old refugee from a leper colony. Despite the possibility of your having matured slightly in the last nine years, that is really what I expect.

However, this sort of thing is popular these days. If you feel your boy can do college work and if you can get him over here and supply him with a thousand dollars a year, we will give him a chance. Enclosed is an application for Ho-Jon to complete.

Sincerely,
James Lodge
Dean, Androscoggin College

"Boys," said Hawkeye, "it's going to cost us at least five or six grand, figuring travel and one thing or another."

"I know we'll get it up, but I don't know how," said Duke.

Dago Red entered. He had some pictures he had taken of the Swampmen during the winter. At the time Trapper John had been sporting a beard and a large crop of unbarbered hair. Several of the pictures were of Trapper John.

"Look at The Hairy Ape," said Duke.

72

"No," said Red, "he doesn't look like The Hairy Ape. With that thin, ascetic face and the beard and the piercing eyes, he almost looks like our Blessed Saviour."

Taking another look, he crossed himself and thought better of it.

"If that's what He looks like," said the Duke, "I'm gonna try Buddha."

"Lemme see that picture," said Hawkeye Pierce.

He looked. "By Jesus, it does look like Him," he agreed and lapsed into pensive silence.

A while later Hawkeye sat up, lit a butt, and said, "Hey, Trapper, how fast can you grow that beard back?"

"Couple weeks. What do you have in mind?"

"Money for Ho-Jon."

"How's that Yankee growin' a beard gonna get money for Ho-Jon?" asked Duke.

"Easy. We'll get a good picture of him, have copies made, and sell actual photographs of Jesus Christ at a buck a throw. If we make out with that, he can make a few personal appearances."

Trapper looked interested. "Always knew I'd make good," he said, "but I never thought I'd get to the top so fast."

"I'm movin' to another tent," wailed the Duke. "You crazy bastards are gonna get me in trouble."

"Now wait a minute, boys. You can't do this," pleaded Dago Red.

"Maybe not, Red," answered Hawkeye, "but we gotta get some money. This idea is crazy, but there are a lot of screwballs in an army. Trapper's picture will sell, and a lot of people will buy them for laughs and souvenirs. It won't hurt anybody, and it's a good cause. All we gotta do is work out the details."

Two weeks later the beard had grown, pictures had been taken and seven thousand prints made. Trapper John spent two days autographing them. Dago Red was frantic. They

73

were ready for action. The enlisted men were fond of the Swampmen and were delighted to buy pictures of Trapper J. Jesus Christ McIntyre at a dollar a copy.

"We got us two bills," said Duke who in a day had unloaded 200 copies. "Let's go to Seoul and see if we can run it up in a crap game."

"Hell with that," declared Hawkeye. "If tomorrow is quiet, we'll get a truck from the motor pool and hit the sawdust trail."

At eight o'clock the next morning, the Swampmen ate a substantial breakfast. A truck was obtained. A large cross that Hawkeye had commissioned the supply sergeant to construct was hidden under blankets in the rear. Also hidden under the blankets was a nearly naked, bearded, long haired, fuzzy chested Trapper John, two dozen cans of beer and a thermos jug full of ice. In the cab were six thousand eight hundred photographs bearing the signature: *Jesus Christ.*

They visited medical corps collecting stations, battalion aid stations, artillery units, and other outfits. As they approached, the cross was erected behind the cab of the truck with straps binding Trapper John in the proper and accepted position. Hawkeye was at the wheel. After a turn or two around an outfit they halted. At nearly every stop, as Trapper peered beseechingly at the sky, an officer would step forward and demand, "What the hell is going on here?"

"Passion play," Hawkeye would explain. "Raising some dough to send our houseboy to college. For a buck you get an autographed picture of the Man, himself, or a reasonable facsimile thereof."

Trade was brisk. No one seemed to object to the performance until, late in the afternoon, they hit a Mississippi National Guard outfit. By this time Trapper, spending most of the hot day hidden beneath blankets in the rear of the truck, had consumed a lot of beer. He was still hot and still dehydrated despite the beer, however, when he once again assumed his position on the cross, so while Duke peddled autographed pictures, Hawkeye surreptitiously slipped Trapper a sip from a cool tin of brew. Four Guardsmen, attempting to obtain samples of wood from the cross as souvenirs, and observing this, became indignant. The indignation spread. The Swampmen departed in haste and returned to the 4077th, where the day's take was found to be a satisfying three grand.

That night they decided to push their luck. The moon was bright, making helicopter flying possible, so the chopper pilots of the Air Rescue Squadron were enlisted. Hawkeye and Duke, with pictures, traveled by jeep to prearranged points where troops were in fair quantity. They announced the availability of personally autographed photographs of Jesus Christ, and their timing was perfect. At each point, as the sales talk ended, a brilliant phosphorus flare would be lit, and a helicopter would appear. Spread-eagled on a cross dangling beneath the chopper and illuminated by the eerie light of the flare was the loinclothed, skinny, bearded, long haired, and pretty well stoned Trapper John.

Any good act swings. The pictures sold. Back in The Swamp at 1:00 A.M. the loot was counted again. They had six thousand five hundred dollars.

"Let it go at that," said the Duke. "We got what we need."

The next day Hawkeye Pierce arranged for five thousand dollars to be sent to his father, Benjamin Franklin Pierce, Sr., along with a note:

Dear Dad:
    This five thousand dollars is for my friend, Ho-Jon, to go to Androscoggin College. Look after him and the money until I get home.

So long,
Hawkeye

Within the next month Hawkeye received two letters. The first was from his father:

Dear Hawkeye:
    I deposited five thousand dollars in the Port Waldo Trust Company for Ho-Jon. How come you can send some foreigner to college and leave me to bail your brothers out of jail? I always encouraged you to go to school, and now look what happens. Your brother Joe got took up for drunken driving. Mother is well.

Your father,
Benjy Pierce

The second letter was from the Dean of Androscoggin College, Dr. James Lodge:

Dear Hawkeye:
    We have received Ho-Jon's application, and his record appears to be outstanding, although somewhat unusual. The letter accompanying his application was particularly impressive and influenced our decision to accept him. My suggestion that you might have written it for him was quickly squelched by members of the English Department who remember you.
    Yesterday a truckful of lobster bait, departing from campus roads, drove directly to the front door of the administration building. A large gentleman, who identified himself as your father, disembarked and gave us one thousand dollars on account for Ho-Jon. We killed a pint of Old Bantam Whiskey which he happened to have with him. Today I have a big head, and the building smells like a lobster boat. Nevertheless, we look forward to Ho-Jon's arrival.

Very truly yours,
James Lodge
Dean, Androscoggin College

The money left over bought clothes and tickets for Ho-Jon.

On August 20, 1952, he concluded his duties as Swampboy. He arrived at Androscoggin College on September 10. Soon after, Hawkeye Pierce's old fraternity, assured by Hawkeye that Ho-Jon's prep school education had included martini mixing and crapshooting, pledged him.

8 Trapper John McIntyre had grown up in a house adjacent to one of suburban Boston's finest country clubs. His parents were members, and, at the age of seventeen, he was one of the better junior golfers in Massachusetts.

Golf had not played a prominent role in Hawkeye Pierce's formative years. Ten miles from Crabapple Cove, however, there was a golf course patronized by the summer resident group. During periods when the pursuit of clams and lobsters was unprofitable, Hawkeye had found employment as a caddy. From time to time he had played with the other caddies and, one year, became the caddy champion of the Wawenock Harbor Golf Club. This meant that he was the only one of ten kids who could break ninety.

In college Hawkeye's obligation to various scholarships involved attention to other games, but during medical school, his internship and his residency he had played golf as often as possible. Joining a club had been out of the question, and even payment of green fees was economically unsound.

Therefore he developed a technique which frequently allowed him the privilege of playing some public and a number of unostentatious private courses. He would walk confidently into a pro shop, smile, comment upon the nice condition of the course, explain that he was just passing through and that he was Joe, Dave or Jack Somebody, the pro from Dover. This resulted, about eight times out of ten, in an invitation to play for free. If forced into conversation, he became the pro from Dover, New Hampshire, Massachusetts, New Jersey, England, Ohio, Delaware, Tennessee, or Dover-Foxcroft, Maine, whichever seemed safest.

There was adequate room to hit golf balls at the Double Natural, and with the arrival of spring Trapper and Hawkeye had commissioned the chopper pilots to bring clubs and balls from Japan. Then they had established a practice range of sorts in the field behind the officers' latrine. The Korean houseboys were excellent ball shaggers, so the golfing Swampmen spent much of their free time hitting wood and iron shots. They began to suspect that if they ever got on a real course they'd burn it up, at least from tee to green, but that possibility seemed as remote as their chances of winning the Nobel prize for medicine.

The day after The Second Coming of Trapper John, however, a young Army private, engaged in training maneuvers near Kokura, Japan, had, when a defective grenade exploded, been struck in the chest by a fragment. X-rays revealed blood in the right pleural cavity, which contains the lung, the possible presence of blood within the pericardium, which surrounds the heart, and a metallic foreign body which seemed, to the Kokura doctors in attendance, to be within the heart itself.

Two factors complicated the case: (1) there was no chest surgeon in the area and (2) the soldier's father was a member of Congress. Had it not been for the second complication, the patient would have been sent to the Tokyo Army Hospital where the problem could have been handled promptly and capably.

When informed immediately of his son's injury, however, the Congressman consulted medical friends and was referred to a widely known Boston surgeon whose advice in this matter would be the best available. The Boston surgeon told the Congressman that, regardless of what the Army had to say, the man to take care of his son was Dr. John F. X. McIntyre, now stationed at the 4077th MASH somewhere in Korea. Congressmen make things move. Within hours a jet was flying out of Kokura and then a chopper was whirling out of Seoul, bearing X-rays, a summary of the case, and orders for Captain McIntyre and anyone else he needed to get to Kokura in a hurry.

Unaware of all this excitement, Trapper John and Hawkeye were hitting a few on the driving range when the chopper from Seoul arrived. They first heard, then saw, it approaching, but as they were off duty and it was coming from the south, anyway, they ignored it. Trapper, still taken with his new image, had not gotten around to shaving his beard or having his hair cut, and he was bending over and teeing up a ball when the pilot, directed to them, walked up.

"Captain McIntyre?" the pilot said.

"What?" Trapper John said, straightening up and turning to face his visitor.

"God!" the pilot said, stunned by his first look at the man whose importance had set a whole chain of command from generals down to clerk-typists into action.

"His son," Hawkeye said. "Would you like to buy an autographed picture for . . . ?"

"*You're* Captain McIntyre?" the pilot said.

"That's what the Army calls me," Trapper said. "Take off your shirt, stick out your tongue and tell me about the pain."

Completely bewildered now, the pilot silently handed over the white envelope containing orders and the explanatory

80

letter from General Hamilton Hartington Hammond and with it the large brown manila envelope containing the X-rays of the chest of the Congressman's son. Trapper read the first and handed them over to Hawkeye and then, as Trapper held the X-rays up to the sunlight, the two looked at them.

"I don't think the goddam thing's in his heart," said Hawkeye, without great assurance.

"Course it isn't," affirmed Trapper John, "but let's not annoy the Congressman. Let us leave for Kokura immediately, with our clubs."

Delaying only long enough to clear it with Henry, they lugged their clubs to the chopper, boosted them in and climbed in after them. At Seoul, Kimpo airport was shrouded with fog and rain, which did not prevent the chopper from landing but which precluded the takeoff of the C-47 scheduled to take them to Kokura. To pass the time in pleasant company, the two surgeons ambled over to the Officers' Club where, after the covey of Air Force people at the bar got over the initial shock, they made the visitors welcome.

"But you guys are a disgrace," said one, after the fourth round. "You can't expect the Air Force to deliver such items to Japan."

"Our problem," Hawkeye explained, "is that right now we've got the longest winning streak in the history of military medicine going, so we don't dare get shaved or shorn. What else can you suggest?"

"Well, we might at least dress you up a little," one of the others said.

"I'm partial to English flannel," Hawkeye said.

"Imported Irish tweed," Trapper said.

The flyboys had recently staged a masquerade party in their club and they still had a couple of Papa-San suits. Papa-San suits take their name from the elderly Korean gentlemen

81

who sport them, and they are long, flowing robes of white or black, topped off by tall hats that look like bird cages.

At 2:00 A.M., Trapper and Hawkeye climbed aboard the C-47, resplendent in their white drapery and bird cages, their clubs over their shoulders. Five hours later they disembarked at Kokura into bright sunlight, found the car with 25th STA-TION HOSPITAL emblazoned on its side, crawled into the back and awakened the driver.

"Garrada there," the sergeant said.

"What?" Trapper said.

"He's from Brooklyn," Hawkeye said. "He wants us to vacate this vehicle."

"I said garrada there," the sergeant said, "or I'll . . ."

"What's the matter?" Trapper said. "You're supposed to pick up the two pros who are gonna operate on the Congressman's son, aren't you?"

"What?" the sergeant said. "You mean *you* guys are the *doctors?*"

"You betcher ever-lovin' A, buddy-boy," Hawkeye said.

"Poor kid," the sergeant said. "Goddam army . . ."

"Look sergeant," Trapper said, "if that spleen of yours is bothering you, we'll remove it right here. Otherwise, let's haul ass."

"Goddam army," the sergeant said.

"That's right," Hawkeye said, "and on the way fill us in on the local golfing facilities. We gotta operate this kid and then get in at least eighteen holes."

The sergeant followed the path of least resistance. On the way he informed the Swampmen that there was a good eighteen hole course not far from the hospital but that, as the Kokura Open was starting the next day, the course was closed to the public.

"So that means we've got a big decision to make," Trapper said.

"What's that?" Hawkeye said.

"The way I see it," Trapper said, for the benefit of the sergeant, "we can operate on this kid and then qualify for this Kokura Open, or we can qualify first and then operate on this kid, if he's still alive."

"Goddam army," the sergeant said.

"Decisions, decisions, decisions," Hawkeye said. "After all, *we* didn't hit the kid in the chest with that grenade."

"Right!" Trapper said. "And it's not *our* chest."

"It's not even our kid," Hawkeye said. "He belongs to some Congressman."

"Yeah," Trapper said, "but let's operate on him first anyway. Then we'll be nice and relaxed to qualify. We wouldn't want to blow that."

"Good idea," Hawkeye said.

"Goddam, goddam army," the sergeant said.

Delivered to the front entrance of the 28th Station Hospital, Trapper and Hawkeye entered and approached the reception desk. Behind it sat a pretty WAC, whose big blue eyes opened like morning glories when she looked up and saw the apparitions before her.

"Nice club you've got here, honey," said Hawkeye. "Where's the pro shop?"

"What?" she said.

"What time's the bar open?" Trapper said.

"What?" she said.

"You got any caddies available?" Hawkeye said.

"What?" she said.

"Look, honey," Trapper said. "Don't keep saying 'what.' Just say 'yes' instead."

"That's right," Hawkeye said, "and you'll be surprised how many friends you'll make in this man's army."

"Yes," she said.

"That's better," Trapper said. "So where's the X-ray department?"

"Yes," she said.

They wandered down the main hallway, people turning to look at them as they passed, until they came to the X-ray department. They walked in, put their clubs in a corner and sat down. They put their feet on the radiologist's desk and lighted cigarettes.

"Don't set fire to your beard," Hawkeye cautioned Trapper John.

"Can't," Trapper said. "Had it fire-proofed."

"What the . . . ?" somebody in the gathering circle of interested X-ray technicians started to say.

"All right," Trapper said. "Somebody trot out the latest pictures of this kid with the shell fragment in his chest."

No one moved.

"Snap it up!" yelled Hawkeye. "We're the pros from Dover, and the last pictures we saw must be forty-eight hours old by now."

Without knowing why, a confused technician produced the X-rays. The pros perused them carefully.

"Just as we thought," said Trapper. "A routine problem."

"Yeah," Hawkeye said. "They must have a hair trigger on the panic button here. Where's the patient?"

"Ward Six," somebody answered.

"Take us there."

Led to Ward Six, the pros politely asked the nurse if they might see the patient. The poor girl, having embarked from the States many months before fully prepared in her mind for any tortures the enemy might inflict upon her, was unprepared for this.

"I don't know," she said. "I don't think I can allow you to see him without the permission of Major Adams."

"Adams?" Trapper said. "John Adams?"

"Adams?" Hawkeye said. "John Quincy Adams?"

"No. George Adams."

"Never heard of him," Trapper said. "Come on now, nice nurse-lady. Let's see the kid."

They followed the hapless nurse into the ward and she led them to the patient. A brief examination revealed that, although the boy did have a two-centimeter shell fragment and a lot of blood in his right chest and that removal of both was relatively urgent, he was in no immediate danger. His confidence and well-being were not particularly enhanced, however, by the bearded, robed, big-hatted character who had dumped a bag of golf clubs at the foot of his bed and had then started to listen to his chest.

"Have no fear, Trapper John is here," Hawkeye assured him in a loud voice, and then, privately, he whispered in the patient's ear: "Don't worry, son. This is Captain McIntyre, and he's the best chest surgeon in the Far East and maybe the whole U.S. Army. He's gonna fix you up easy. Your Daddy saw to that."

When they asked, the Swampmen were told by the nurse that blood had been typed and that an adequate supply had been cross-matched. They picked up their clubs and, following directions, headed for the operating area where they found their way barred by a fierce Captain of the Army Nurse Corps.

"Stop, right where you are!" she ordered.

"Don't get mad, m'am," Hawkeye said. "All we want is our starting time."

"Get out!" she screamed.

"Look, mother," Trapper said. "I'm the pro from Dover. Me and my greenskeeper want to crack that kid's chest and get out to the course. Find the gas-passer and tell him to pre-medicate the patient, and find this Major Adams so he can get his spiel over with. Also, while you're at it, I need a can of beans and my greenskeeper here wants ham and eggs. It's now eight o'clock. I want to work at nine. Hop to it!"

She did, much to her own surprise. Breakfast was served, followed immediately by Major Adams who, after his initial shock, adjusted to the situation when it developed that all three had a number of mutual friends in the medical dodge.

"I don't know about the C.O., though," Major Adams said, meaning the Commanding Officer.

"Who is he?" Hawkeye said.

"Colonel Ruxton P. Merrill. Red-neck R.A. all the way."

"Don't worry about him," Trapper said. "We'll handle him."

At nine o'clock the operation started. At nine-oh-three Colonel Merrill, having heard about the unusual invasion of his premises, stormed into the operating room. He was without gown, cap or mask, so Hawkeye, deploring the break in the antiseptic techniques prescribed for OR's, turned to the circulating nurse and ordered: "Get that dirty old man out of this operating room!"

"I'm Colonel Merrill!" yelled Colonel Merrill.

Hawkeye turned and impaled him on an icy stare. "Beat it, Pop. If this chest gets infected, I'll tell the Congressman on you."

After that there was no further excitement, and the operation, as the Swampmen had surmised, turned out to be routine. Within forty-five minutes the definitive work was done, and only the chest closure remained.

When the operation had started, the anesthesiologist of the 25th Station Hospital had been so busy getting the patient asleep in order to meet the deadline imposed by the pros from Dover that he had not been introduced. Furthermore, he had not seen them without their masks—nor had they seen him—but when he had a chance to settle down and relax, the shell fragment and the blood having been removed to the perceptible betterment of the patient's condition, he wrote at the top of his anesthesia record the name "Hawkeye Pierce" in the space labeled "First Assistant." He wrote it with assurance and with pleasure.

The anesthesiologist was Captain Ezekiel Bradbury (Me Lay) Marston, V, of Spruce Harbor, Maine. In Spruce Harbor, Maine, the name Marston is synonymous with romantic visions of the past—specifically clipper ships—and money. The first to bear the name captained a clipper, bought it and built three more. The second commanded the flagship of the fleet and bought four more. Number III was skipper of the *Spruce Harbor*, which went down with all hands off Hatteras some three years after number IV had been born in its Captain's cabin forty miles south of Cape Horn. Number V was Me Lay Marston, the only swain in Spruce Harbor High who could say, "Me lay, you lay?" and parlay such a simple, unimaginative approach into significant success with the young females of the area.

Hawkeye Pierce thought of it first, and last, but Me Lay Marston had also gone around for a while with the valedictorian of the Class of '41 at Port Waldo High School. In November, 1941, after Spruce Harbor beat Port Waldo 38–0, Pierce and Marston engaged in a fist fight which neither won decisively. In subsequent years they belonged to the same fraternity at Androscoggin College, played on the same football team, attended the same medical school and, during internship, they shared the same room. Me Lay was an usher when Hawkeye Pierce married the valedictorian, and Hawkeye provided a similar service when Me Lay did the same for the Broad from Eagle Head, whom Hawkeye had also dated for a while.

During his adolescence and earliest manhood, Me Lay had been proud of his name. Now, circumstances having forced him to correct his behavior, he was merely resigned to it. By 1952, however, he had not been addressed as Me Lay for three years. He had not seen Hawkeye Pierce for three years.

So on a bright, warm day in Kokura the fifth in a series of Captain Marstons looked up from his chart and asked, "May I have the surgeon's name, please?"

Hawkeye Pierce answered, "He's the pro from Dover and I'm the Ghost of Smoky Joe."

"Save that crap for someone else, you stupid clamdigger," answered Captain Marston.

The surgeons stopped. The first assistant leaned over and looked at the anesthesia chart and saw his name. He knew the writing and recognized the writer. He took it in his stride.

"Me Lay, I'd like you to meet Trapper John."

"The real Trapper John? Your cousin who threw you the pass and went on to greater fame on the Boston & Maine?"

"The one and only," affirmed Hawkeye.

"Trapper, you are in bad company," said Me Lay, "but I'll be happy to shake your hand if you'll hurry up and get that chest closed. You still workin' the trains?"

"Planes mostly. May take a crack at rickshas. You still employing the direct approach?"

"No, not since I married the Broad from Eagle Head. I've been out of action now for four years."

"Then what the hell do you do around here?" asked Hawkeye. "It doesn't look like you're very busy. You mean to tell us you don't chase the local scrunch?"

"I don't seem to be interested in it from that angle. The first month I was here all I did was wind my watch and evacuate my bladder. Now I'm taking a course in Whorehouse Administration."

"Under the auspices of the Army's Career Management Plan?" inquired Trapper.

"No, all on my own."

"It was Yankee drive and ingenuity that built the Marston fortune," Hawkeye pointed out. "I'm proud of you, Me Lay. Where are you taking the course?"

"At Dr. Yamamoto's Finest Kind Pediatric Hospital and Whorehouse," Captain Marston informed him.

"Cut the crap, Me Lay. This sounds like too much even for you."

"I'm serious. This guy practices pediatrics, has a little hospital and runs a whorehouse, all in the same building."

"What are you? A pimp?"

"No. I keep the books, inspect the girls and take care of some of the kids in the hospital. Occasionally I tend bar and act as bouncer. A guy needs well rounded training to embark on a career such as this."

The chest got closed, despite the conversation. In the dressing room the Swampmen got back into their Papa-San suits and continued the reunion with Me Lay Marston.

"What's with this Colonel Merrill?" asked Trapper.

"Red-neck R.A. all the way," Captain Marston said. "He'll give you a bad time if you let him."

A messenger entered and stated that Captains Pierce and McIntyre were to report to the colonel's office immediately. Me Lay gave them the address of the FKPH&W and suggested that they meet him there at seven that evening for dinner and whatnot.

"OK," Hawkeye said, and then he turned to the messenger waiting to guide them to the colonel's office. "Got any caddy carts?"

"What?" the messenger said.

Sighing, they slung their clubs over their shoulders and followed the guide. The colonel was temporarily occupied elsewhere, so rather than just sit there during his absence and read his mail, the Swampmen decided to practice putting on his carpet.

"You men are under arrest," the colonel boomed, when he stormed onto the scene.

"Quiet!" Trapper said. "Can't you see I'm putting?"

"Why, you . . ."

"Let's get down to bare facts, Colonel," Hawkeye said. "Probably even you know this case didn't demand our presence. Be that as it may, your boys blew it. We bailed it out, and a Congressman is very much interested. We figure this kid needs about five days of postop care from us, and we also figure to play in the Kokura Open. If that ain't okay with you, we'll get on the horn to a few Congressmen."

"Or one, anyway," Trapper John said.

It was mean but not too bold, and they knew it would work. They took their clubs and walked out. At the front door of the hospital they found the car which had brought them from the airport. It was the colonel's car, and the sergeant was lounging nearby, awaiting the colonel. Trapper John and Hawkeye got into the front seat.

"Hey, wait a minute," the sergeant said.

"The colonel is lending us his car," Hawkeye informed the Sergeant. "We'll give it back after the Open."

"That's right," Trapper said. "He wants you to go in now, and write some letters for the Congressman's son."

"Goddam army," the sergeant said.

They drove to the golf course and parked, unloaded their clubs and walked into the pro shop. Although most of the golfers were members of the American and British armed forces, the pro was Japanese and he greeted the appearance of two Korean Papa-Sans with evident hostility.

"How do we qualify for the Open?" asked Hawkeye.

"There twenty-five dollar entry fee," the pro informed him, eyeing him coldly.

"But I'm the pro from Dover, and this here is my assistant," announced Hawkeye, handing the Japanese his Maine State Golf Association handicap card.

"Ah, so," the Japanese hissed.

"We're just in from visiting relatives in Korea," Trapper informed him. "Our clothes got burned up. We can't get any new ones until we win some dough in your tournament."

"Ah, so," hissed the pro, much relieved, and he promptly supplied them with golf shoes and two female caddies.

With the wide-eyed girls carrying the clubs, they trekked to the first tee. There, waiting to tee off, they were taking a few practice swings, to the amusement of all in their vicinity, when they observed four British officers, one of them a colonel, approaching. In a matter of minutes two things became evident. Judged by his own practice swings the British colonel was not on leave from his country's Curtis Cup team, and judged by the disdain evident on his face when he eyed the Swampmen he was not in favor of any Papa-Sans sharing the golf course with him.

"Damn this get-up," Hawkeye was saying to Trapper. "It doesn't do much for my backswing."

"Good," Trapper said, increasing the awkwardness of his own efforts.

"What do you mean, good?" Hawkeye said.

"Keep your voice down," Trapper said, "because I think we're about to hook a live one."

"See here, you two!" the British colonel bleated, walking up to them at that moment. "I don't know who you think you are, but I think . . ."

"Think again," Trapper said.

"I want you to know I'm Colonel Cornwall . . ."

"Cornwallis?" Hawkeye said. "I thought we fixed your wagon at Yorktown."

"I said Cornwall."

"Lovely there in the spring," Trapper said. "Rhododendrons and all that."

"Now see here!" the colonel said, red in the face now. "I don't know what you're doing here, but rather than make an issue of it, if you'll just step aside and allow us to tee off . . ."

"Look, Corny," Hawkeye said. "You just calm down, or we'll tee off on *you*."

"I'll tell you what we'll do, Colonel," Trapper said. "You look like a sporting chap, so to settle this little difficulty in a sporting way, we'll both play you a ten pound Nassau."

"I beg your pardon?"

"You heard him," Hawkeye said.

"Excuse me a moment," the colonel said, and he turned and rejoined his companions to get their opinion of the proposition.

"What do you think?" Hawkeye said.

"We got him," Trapper said, manufacturing as awkward a swing as he could without making it too obvious.

"Here he comes now," Hawkeye said.

"All right," the colonel said. "You're on, and we'll be watching every shot you hit."

The Swampmen hit drives designed to get the ball in play, with no attempt at distance, and they were down the middle about 225 yards. Trapper reached the green in two and got his par four. Hawkeye hit a nice five-iron but misjudged the distance and was long, hit a wedge back but missed a five-footer and took a bogey.

The second hole was a short par three that gave them no trouble. Both bogied three and four, however, as it became clear that driving range experience at the Double Natural had sharpened their hitting ability but done little for their judgment of distance or their putting. Nevertheless, the girl caddies were quite impressed, particularly by Trapper John, whose every move they watched with rapt fascination.

Approaching the seventh, a par five, they were both three over par, and as the day was getting warmer, Trapper took off the long, flowing top of his Papa-San suit and his hat. This left him with long hair, a beard, a bare torso, and long, flowing trousers, and seemed to move him up another notch in the eyes of the girls.

On the seventh, he was down the middle a good 260, with Hawkeye not far behind him. Hawkeye's second shot wasn't much, however, and he had a full five-iron left. Then Trapper cranked out an awesome two-wood with a slight tail-end hook which hit the hard fairway, bounced over a trap, and came to rest within two feet of the pin.

"Jesus!" exclaimed Hawkeye. The caddies, hearing this,

looked knowingly at each other, and it dawned on the Swampmen what their mounting excitement was all about. Happily, Hawkeye had several of the autographed pictures in his wallet and, with a grand gesture, he bestowed complimentary copies upon the girls who, their suspicions confirmed, were overcome. Hawkeye had to lead them aside to calm them down, explaining as best he could that the Master's game was a little rusty and that He wanted to get in at least eighteen holes before making His comeback generally known.

"These bimboes," he explained to Trapper, approaching the eighth tee, "are on a real Christian kick, so don't disappoint them."

Trapper grabbed his driver, winced and looked at his hands. "Goddam nail holes," he complained.

The rest of the way around, Trapper played even par on the not too difficult and not too long course to finish with a seventy-three. Hawkeye couldn't figure the greens and found himself needing a ten-footer on the eighteenth for a seventy-eight. Trapper blessed the ball and the cup before Hawkeye essayed the putt, which went in like it had eyes. The caddies, bowing their way out, departed to spread the word.

"Now," Trapper said, "let's prepare to lighten Corny's load a little. If that hacker breaks eighty I'll take it to the World Court."

The Swampmen, with Trapper back in full uniform, found the bar. They were on their second Scotch when they noticed the Japanese faces peeking through the window and then Colonel Cornwall and his three colleagues pushing their way through the crowd at the door.

"I say now," the colonel was saying, brushing himself off. "Does anyone know what this is all about?"

"Ah, yes," Hawkeye said, motioning toward Trapper, who was bowing toward the faces at the window and door. "Mighty High Religious Personage is greeting followers."

"Of course, of course," the colonel was saying now, starting to rock with laughter. "I say! That's rather droll, isn't it?"

"What's that, sir?" one of his colleagues asked.

"Chap here," he said, nodding toward Trapper. "Why, the chap here's portraying John the Baptist!"

"Colonel," Hawkeye said, handing him one of the autographed pictures, "you can't tell the players without a scorecard."

"Oh, I say!" the colonel was roaring now. "That *is* good, isn't it? I *do* get it now. Say, you chaps, do have a drink on me. Oh, I say!"

The Swampmen had several drinks on him and, when they got around to comparing cards, the colonel, who had shot an eighty-two, paid up willingly.

"Corny," Hawkeye heard himself saying, "how about you and these other gentlemen joining us for dinner at Dr. Yamamoto's Finest Kind Pediatric Hospital and Whorehouse?"

"Oh, I say!" the colonel said. "That sounds like sport!"

Shortly after 7:00 P.M., Me Lay Marston, idly sipping a martini in the bar of the FKPH&W, heard a commotion outside. Going to the door, he found Hawkeye, the British contingent and then Trapper John bringing up the rear. Trapper was trying to disentangle himself from the converts and the just curious.

"Me Lay," Trapper said, when he got inside, "I've had enough of this. Get me a pair of scissors and a razor."

In time Trapper John was shaved, shorn and showered, and dinner was solicitously served by the young ladies. While the visitors sipped after-dinner cordials, Me Lay excused himself to make his rounds at the adjoining hospital. In a few minutes he returned with a worried look.

"What had you guys planned for tonight?" he asked.

"Well," answered Trapper, "we thought we'd get some . . ."

"How about looking at a kid for me?"

"Look, Me Lay," Hawkeye said, "you're supposed to be the intern in this . . ."

"Shut up, and come look at this kid."

"What's the story?" asked Trapper.

"Well, one of our girls got careless, and two days ago she gave birth to an eight pound Japanese-American male."

"What's wrong with him?"

"Every time we feed him, it either comes right back up or he coughs and turns blue and has a helluva time."

"We don't have to see him," Trapper said. "Call that half-assed Army Hospital and tell them to be ready to put some lipiodal in this kid's esophagus and take X-rays."

"But it's ten-thirty at night. We can't get everybody out for a civilian. They won't do it."

"How much you wanna bet, Me Lay?" inquired Hawkeye Pierce. "Get on the horn and tell them the pros from Dover are on their way with a patient. Better tell the OR to crank itself up, because I got a feeling that you're going to pass some gas while I help Trapper close a tracheo-esophageal fistula."

"Oh, I say," Colonel Cornwall wanted to know, "what's that?"

"It's a hole between the esophagus and the trachea, where it doesn't belong," Hawkeye explained.

"And you chaps can repair that?"

"Well," said Me Lay. "We can try."

At the 25th Station Hospital, the Officer of the Day received a call from Captain Marston saying that an emergency was coming in for X-rays. Soon after, Hawkeye and Trapper, in Papa-San suits and followed by Me Lay carrying the baby, entered the X-ray department.

Captain Banks, the O.D., arrived and asked, "What's this all about?"

"It's all about this baby," Hawkeye informed him. "We want to X-ray him and we want to do it right now, and we do not wish to be engaged in useless conversation by officious military types, of which you look like one to me."

"But, we can't . . ."

Hawkeye sat Captain Banks on the edge of a desk and handed him the phone.

"Be nice, Captain. Call the X-ray technician. If you give us any kind of a bad time, me and Trapper John are going to clean your clock. We are frustrated lovers and quite dangerous."

Captain Banks called. While awaiting the technician, Trapper and Me Lay placed a small catheter in the baby's esophagus. A few minutes later, radio-opaque oil was injected through the catheter. It revealed the abnormal opening between the esophagus and the trachea but no significant narrowing of the esophagus. This meant that anything the baby ate could go into his lungs but that, happily, once the opening was closed, the espohagus would be able to accommodate the passage of food. It required careful preparation, proper anesthesia, early and competent surgery and good luck.

"Me Lay, let's you and me get a needle into a vein," Trapper said, and then, turning to Captain Banks, he said, "You there, in the shiny shoes, tell the lab to do a blood count and cross-match a pint. We won't need that much, but it's a term they'll understand. Then tell the OR to get set up for a thoracotomy. We're going to operate in about two hours. Hawkeye, you stick close to Alice, or whatever his name is, and see that he performs efficiently."

The Officer of the Day had no choice but to perform efficiently. The nurses were routed out, not at all pleased at the prospect of operating a second time with the pros from Dover. There was, in fact, outright grumbling which Hawkeye Pierce brought to a rapid conclusion.

"Ladies," he said, "we are sorry to get you out at this time of night. However, we stumbled upon this deal, and we can't walk away from it, no matter whose rules are broken. This baby will die if we don't fix him, so let's all be nice and just think about the baby."

Fortunately, nurses succumb to this kind of pitch. They gave up any show of resistance, particularly after they saw the baby, but Hawkeye caught Captain Banks calling Colonel Merrill.

"Now, Captain," he chided him, "I may give you a few lumps, but first I must call the Finest Kind Pediatric Hospital and Whorehouse."

So doing, he talked to Colonel Cornwall, explained their situation and made a few suggestions. Fifteen minutes later, as Colonel R. P. Merrill stormed into the hospital, he was met by four British officers who loaded him unceremoniously into their Land Rover and returned to the FKPH&W.

After Captain Banks had been stripped naked, and locked in a broom closet by the two Swampmen, the operation was finally started. Me Lay's anesthesia was excellent, the nurses cooperated completely, and Trapper and Hawkeye indulged in none of the by-play that had marked their first local appearance. After an hour and a half of careful work, Trapper had closed the fistula. They shed their gowns and discussed the postoperative care.

"I think we better leave him here," said Trapper. "You can't take care of anything like this in that whorehouse hospital of yours, can you, Me Lay?"

"Not too well, but I don't see how we can keep him here. Merrill will be all over us in the morning."

"Leave the kid here," Hawkeye said. "We'll be in and out and can look after both him and the boy we did this morning. I know how to keep Merrill off our backs."

At 3:00 A.M., back at the FKPH&W, they had a drink with the British officers who told them that Colonel Merrill was upstairs asleep, having been coaxed into having a drink and a sedative.

"But what about when he wakes up?" asked Me Lay.

"Send a naked broad into his room and take some pictures," suggested Hawkeye.

"Oh, I say!" Colonel Cornwall said.

A few minutes later, Colonel Merrill began to stir and awaken as the girl joined him in bed. Witnesses to the scene filled the doorway while Trapper John leisurely shot a roll of film.

"I told you so! I told you so!" chanted Hawkeye. "He's a dirty old man. A disgrace to the uniform."

"The blighter should bloody well be cashiered from the service," asserted Colonel Cornwall indignantly.

"I'd say that depends on his behavior from now on," said Trapper John, pocketing the film.

The Swampmen were to tee off in the Kokura Open at ten o'clock the next morning. One of Me Lay's assistants was instructed to obtain proper clothing, since they did not wish to wear Papa-San suits forever.

Awakening at 8:00 A.M., weary but determined to be ready for the tournament, they drank coffee, ate steak and eggs served in bed by the ladies of the house, and donned sky blue slacks and golf shirts.

On the way to the course, they visited their two patients. The baby was far from out of the woods, but the Congressman's son was doing well. Before leaving, they entered the colonel's office.

"Where's that dirty old man?" Hawkeye asked the secretary.

The colonel came out, but he didn't roar.

"Colonel," said Hawkeye, "we've qualified for the Kokura Open so we're going to the course. We expect your people to watch that baby we operated on last night like he was the Congressman's grandson, which for all we know he may be. We expect to be notified of any change for the worse, and if we find anything wrong when we come back this afternoon, we'll burn down the hospital."

The Colonel believed them.

They arrived at the golf course at nine-thirty, practiced

putting and chipping, took a few swings and, with their English confreres there to cheer them on, they pronounced themselves ready to go. They weren't. The activities of the previous days, and nights, had taken too much out of them, and by the end of the third day, what with having to check repeatedly on the Congressman's son and the baby, they were hopelessly mired back in the pack.

"I guess that does it," Trapper said, as they sat in the bar at the club. "We might have a chance if three guys dropped dead and a half dozen others came down with echinococcosus."

"What's that?" Colonel Cornwall wanted to know.

"The liver gets so big you can't get your club head back past it," Hawkeye said, "so we've got no chance."

"We're proud of you anyway," the colonel informed them. "You gave it a good go, you did. I must say, though, I shouldn't give up surgery for the professional tour if I were you."

"I guess we figured that out already," Trapper said, "but what I can't figure out is what we're going to do about this baby we're stuck with."

"But you chaps have done all you can," the colonel said.

"No, we haven't," Trapper said. "After the big deal we made saving his life, what do we do now? Leave him in a whorehouse?"

"Leave it to me," Hawkeye said. "I think it'll be safe now to take the kid back to Dr. Yamamoto's Finest Kind Pediatric Hospital and Whorehouse."

They went to the 25th Station Hospital, said good-bye to the Congressman's son who was well on his way to recovery, and picked up their small patient. Riding the Land Rover back to the FKPH&W, Trapper had a thought.

"We oughta name the little bastard," he said.

Hawkeye had considered this problem twenty-four hours earlier. He had even laid a little groundwork.

"I have named him," he said.

"What is it?"

"I'm not sure how much I can con Me Lay Marston into," Hawkeye said, "but the name is Ezekiel Bradbury Marston, VI."

"Oh, I say," Colonel Cornwall said.

"Obviously you are either nuts or you know something," Trapper John said eventually. "Which is it?"

"I know something. I know that Me Lay and the Broad from Eagle Head have one daughter and that's all the kids they're ever going to have. I'll save you the next question. Remember I was away for a while last night? I went to one of those overseas telephone places and called the Broad from Eagle Head, whom I've known longer than Me Lay has. To make a long story short, she agrees that a name like Ezekiel Bradbury Marston must not die!"

"Hawkeye, you are amazing," admired the Colonel.

"For once, I gotta agree," agreed Trapper.

At the FKPH&W, they placed Ezekiel Bradbury Marston, VI, in a laundry basket, left instructions for his care and returned to the bar where they found the unsuspecting parent, Me Lay Marston.

"What are we going to do with this kid, Me Lay?" asked Trapper.

"I don't know."

"Well, Jesus, Me Lay, you're not much of a whorehouse administrator if you don't have some ideas on the subject."

"Good-looking kid," said Hawkeye. "What's his mother like?"

"A nice intelligent girl. She asked me this morning what we'd do with the baby. I've been looking into a few possibilities, but I'll tell you right now there aren't any good ones."

"Too bad. The little chap's half American," said Colonel Cornwall. "Any way to get him to the States?"

"Only one way," said Me Lay.

"What's that?"

"Get somebody to adopt him."

Hawkeye said, "Me Lay, why don't you adopt him?"

Me Lay looked miserable. He lit a cigarette and sipped his drink.

"That idea's been popping into my head ever since we operated on him," he said, finally, "but how can I do it? Am I supposed to call up my wife and say I'm sending home a half-breed bastard from a Japanese whorehouse?"

"You don't have to," Trapper told him. "Hawkeye called your wife last night. The deal's set. All you have to do is arrange the details."

Hesitating only a moment, Me Lay got up, went to the hospital area, picked up the baby and brought him to the bar.

"What's his name, Me Lay?" asked Trapper.

"Gentlemen, meet my son, Ezekiel Bradbury Marston, VI, of Spruce Harbor, Maine."

Late that night a flyboy who'd been in Seoul earlier in the day brought word of increasing action on Old Baldy. The next morning the pros from Dover, having withdrawn from the tournament, but still clad in sky blue slacks and golf shirts, boarded a plane for Seoul.

9 In the middle of a hot, humid and bloody afternoon Lt. Col. Henry Blake finished a bowel resection, assessed the grief in the admitting and preop wards and then stepped outside to smoke, pace back and forth and, about once every ten seconds, look hopefully to the south. From the number and nature of the casualties, and with the privileged information from Radar O'Reilly that the situation on Old Baldy would get worse before it got better, he knew that he—that all of them—were in trouble. Between his looks to the south he swore at the Army for taking two of his three best cutters to Kokura and not getting them back in time.

As he ground out his butt, drew a deep breath and made a half-hearted attempt to square his sagging shoulders, he took a last look down the valley and saw it—a cloud of dust. Henry smiled and, for the first time in twenty-four hours, relaxed because he knew that just ahead of just such a dust cloud had to be a jeep driven by Hawkeye Pierce. Seconds later Hawkeye and Trapper, in sky blue slacks and golf shirts, jumped from the jeep.

"Hail, gallant leader!" Hawkeye said, snapping off a salute.

"The organization looks busy," observed Trapper John to Hawkeye, "so I wonder what its gallant leader is doing, just standing here and dilly-dallying in the sunshine."

"Beats me," Hawkeye said.

"You guys get your asses to work!" yelled Henry.

"Yes, sir," Trapper said, saluting.

"Sure, Henry," Hawkeye said, "but we'd appreciate it if you'd get our clubs out of the jeep and clean them."

They ran for the preop ward where the scene informed them that they were in for the busiest day of their lives. What they were yet to learn was that they, and the entire personnel of the 4077th MASH, were in for the busiest two weeks the Double Natural had ever known. For a full two weeks the wounded would come and keep coming, and for a full two weeks every surgeon and every nurse and every corpsman, as the shifts overlapped, would work from twelve to fourteen to sixteen hours a day, every day, and sometimes some of them would work twenty out of the twenty-four.

It could have been chaos, and it almost was. They came in by helicopter and they came in by ambulance—arteries, lungs, bowels, bladders, livers, spleens, kidneys, larynxes, pharynxes, bones, stomachs. Colonel Blake, the surgeons, Ugly John, Painless Waldowski, who, when he wasn't extracting shattered bone and wiring jaws, was passing gas to back up Ugly John, were in constant hurried communication, trying to maintain some order to the flow. Their objective was to provide each patient with the maximum preparation for and the proper timing of his surgery. This was controlled, of course, by the availability of the operating tables and the surgeons. As each new chopper brought new emergencies, plans and timing constantly had to be changed because some cases had to be moved directly from chopper to admitting ward to OR.

From one flight of choppers the Swampmen found eight new arrivals, all of whom needed maximum and immediate attention. The worst was an unconscious Negro private who was the bearer of a note from the doctor in the Battalion Aid Station. The note stated that the patient had been knocked out when a bunker had collapsed, had awakened and then had slowly subsided into unconsciousness again. This was a neurosurgical problem, but the 4077th had no neurosurgeon because such cases were supposed to be sent to the 6073rd MASH, which had several.

Trapper John looked at the note and then at the boy. He looked in his eyes. The right pupil was dilated and fixed. His pulse was slow, his blood pressure negligible.

"I'm afraid this one has an epidural hematoma," he said. "Duke, haven't you been that route a little?"

"Yeah," Duke said, "but not enough to be a pro."

"You're a pro now," Trapper said.

Duke quickly examined the patient. He found indications of pressure on the brain from blood accumulating between the skull and the outer brain lining.

"Right now," he ordered, "lug this one into the OR."

The Duke ran ahead of the stretcher. In the OR he encountered, fortunately, the boss, chief, honcho, leader and head coach of the operating room nurses, Captain Bridget Mc-Carthy of Boston, Massachusetts.

"Quick, Knocko," he commanded, "y'all get me gloves, knife, hammer, chisel, Gelfoam and a drain."

Captain Bridget McCarthy was maybe thirty-five years old, five feet eight inches of solid maple, and she did not ordinarily tolerate much lip from the Swampmen or her immediate superior, Major Hot Lips Houlihan, either. This last endeared her to the Swampmen who did not call her "Knocko" for nothing, for they knew she could take out any

104

one of them in a head-on. More than anything, however, she was also a nurse who had come specifically to be a nurse, so when Duke gave orders with fire in his eye she asked no questions and said, "Yes, sir."

The right temporal area was quickly shaved and scrubbed, and Duke incised down to the bone. He had no desire to go through the skull with a hammer and chisel, but he also had no choice. The appropriate drills for making burr holes were at the 6073rd with the neurosurgeons, so he did the best he could. With luck, or skill born of need, he cracked a jagged hole in the skull in less than a minute. As he broke through, blood flowed out in a torrent. The torrent quickly diminished to a dribble and then Duke exercised highly commendable surgical wisdom. The wise surgeon, particularly when out of his field, knows when to quit, so Duke refrained from looking for hemorrhage beneath the dura mater. He settled for the drainage of the epidural hemorrhage, and the pressure on the brain was relieved. He stuffed Gelfoam down toward the bleeding site, put in a rubber drain, closed the skin with silk sutures, and the soldier began to stir and moan. As his breathing improved and his pulse picked up, the Duke spake the words that, if they ever name a medical school after him, may be carved in stone over the entrance to the administration building:

"He might make it, even if all I really did was hit him in the head with an axe."

As Duke went, then, to the postop ward to write orders on his patient, Captain Bridget McCarthy went to the other end of the operating tent to find out what the excitement was. The excitement was the patient who'd arrived on the same chopper with the epidural hematoma. Hawkeye had looked at him quickly, found him to be in shock, semiconscious but not, it seemed, in immediate danger. His clothes were saturated with mud, as was his hair, and there was a muddy, bloody bandage around his neck.

"Get that bandage off so I can see what the hell's underneath," Hawkeye told a corpsman, and he went on to the patient on the next stretcher.

The corpsman removed the bandage. The patient turned his head to the left. Blood shot two feet into the air from the hole in his right neck where a mortar fragment had entered. The soldier yelled.

"Mama, Mama!" he yelled. "Oh, Mama, I'm dying!"

It looked like a gushing well, and a fascinated group gathered to watch. As the well crested and the blood descended, it fell on the face of the soldier and into his mouth. He coughed, spraying his rapt audience with blood.

Hawkeye ran over. In haste, and instinctively, he stuck his right index finger down the hole, blocking off the severed common carotid artery. He had stopped the flow of blood, but he had also tied up his right hand, and he wondered: "What the hell do I do now?"

"Bring him to the OR right on this stretcher," he yelled. "I can't take my finger out. Find Ugly John and get his ass in here!"

As Knocko McCarthy followed Hawkeye into the OR, she had no chance to ask questions. Hawkeye was still sounding off orders.

"Start somebody cutting off his clothes . . . Tell the lab to come in with a couple of pints of low titre O, and type and cross match him for five or six more . . . Get somebody to do two cutdowns and start the blood . . . Come to think of it, get somebody to start rounding up donors, and send some cowboys to Seoul for all the goddam blood they can get . . . And get that Christly gas passer in here!"

"I'm here," Ugly John said.

"Good," Hawkeye said. "I guess you'd better get him asleep and a tube in him if you can. His common carotid is cut, and I can't do anything with the son of a bitch jumping all over the place. We haven't got time for any of the preoperative pretties."

106

"Mama, Mama!" the patient was yelling. "I'm dying."

"Hold still," Hawkeye said, "or I'll guarantee it."

Ugly John did a cutdown and got into a vein. He got some blood started, as well as Pentothal and curare, and inserted his intratracheal tube. It was still a toss-up. Although the patient had survived the induction of anesthesia, Hawkeye still had to get the carotid clamped off, and as soon as possible.

"Get help," he ordered Knocko McCarthy. "I gotta keep a finger on this or we lose him, and I can't expose it and get it clamped with one hand."

He tried though. Grabbing a scalpel with his left hand, he enlarged the wound around the bare, dirty right index finger which had to stay in the neck. Next he tried to slide a Kelly clamp down his finger into the wound and clamp the artery, but it didn't work. Then he got a retractor and, managing to hold it in the wound with his left hand, he improved the exposure. He was still in desperate need of help.

"Look, Ug," he said to Ugly John who was busy enough with the anesthesia and the new blood, "grab a Kelly, and from where you are I think you can ride it down my finger, grab, and we'll have this mother under control."

Ugly did as told. Reaching the bottom of the wound, he opened the clamp as wide as he could. Sensing that he was around something substantial, he closed the clamp vigorously, asserting, "I got it! I got it!"

He had clamped the end of Hawkeye's finger. Hawkeye, by reflex, removed his finger—and the blood flew. When it did Hawkeye went back in, but this time with his left index finger, and now, with luck, he was able to get a clamp on the artery.

"I'm OK for now," he told Knocko McCarthy and one of the surgeons from the other shift who came running up with her, "but get the Professor."

Most of the surgeons had some locally acquired experience in the care of arterial injuries, but they were still beginners.

Therefore the Army had sent a Professor of Vascular Surgery from Walter Reed Hospital in Washington to give lessons throughout Korea. Fortune had placed him, at this time, at the Double Natural, and he bailed the patient, and Hawkeye, out.

Trapper John, meanwhile, had delved into a chest and Duke was now occupied with several feet of small bowel which were no longer useful to the owner. Hawkeye returned to the preop ward where Colonel Blake had taken charge.

"What's the score now?" Hawkeye asked.

"A major case on every table and ten more that are bad and about thirty that can wait till things quiet down."

"Who's ready?"

"That one over there," said Henry, pointing.

That one turned out to be a very black Negro who was one of Ethiopia's contributions to the UN forces. Hawkeye repaired the damage to the liver and bowel there just in time to assist Trapper John who had gone into another chest. From Trapper he went to help Duke remove the right kidney and a section of colon belonging to a Corporal Ian MacGregor.

"What type we got here?" Hawkeye asked the Duke.

"Don't y'all know you're operating on a member of Princess Patricia's Canadian Light Infantry?" the Duke said.

"Finest kind," Hawkeye said.

That was the way they played it, day after day. As soon as someone finished a case he had to assist elsewhere until another case of his own was brought in. Then, briefed by Colonel Blake, he'd step in and do his best. When the last of the serious cases was allotted, the surgeons, as they became free, would start working on the minor things—debridement of extremity wounds, some with fractures, some requiring an amputation of a finger, a toe, a foot or a leg, but minor as compared with what had gone before. Meanwhile they, and everyone else, would listen for, and dread, the sound of the six o'clock chopper.

The six o'clock chopper, either morning or evening, was always unwelcome because the very fact that the pilot was risking the trip in half-daylight meant that the soldiers lying in the pods were seriously wounded. So twice each day, at dawn and at dusk, as six o'clock approached, everyone—surgeons, nurses, lab technicians, corpsmen, cooks and mostly Lt. Col. Henry Blake—would listen, and during the time of the Great Deluge, they would hear, not one six o'clock chopper but three or four.

"What the hell is going on up there, anyway?" Colonel Blake asked no one in particular one 6:00 P.M., the roar of the choppers filling the postop ward, where the colonel was assessing results with the Swampmen.

"The Chinks," Trapper John said, "are obviously holding a Gold Star Mothers membership drive."

"And it's up to us," Hawkeye said, "to stamp out that organization, so let's get to it."

"Right," Duke said. "We can fix 'em just as fast as they can shoot 'em."

"Right, hell," Henry said. "You guys can't go on like this forever. You haven't had any sleep."

"Right," Duke said.

"How the hell do you feel?" Henry said.

"Better than the patients," Duke said.

"Then what the hell are you doing, standing around here?" Henry said.

The new group was truly international. Hawkeye drew a Turk, and repaired his lacerated colon. Duke took off the right leg of a Puerto Rican kid, portions of whose femur, shattered by a mortar up on Pork Chop Hill, had punctured the chest of his fox hole buddy, who was now on the next table under Trapper's knife. When Trapper finished there, he closed the ruptured diaphragm of a Chinese prisoner of

109

war, while Duke assisted the Professor of Vascular Surgery who was trying to save the left leg of a Netherlands private by fashioning an arterial graft out of a segment of vein from the other leg, and Hawkeye, with Pete Rizzo assisting him, went into the belly of an Australian.

"Dammit," he said, after about a half hour of it, "we just need more hands."

"I know," Pete Rizzo said, "but I only got two."

"Knocko!"

"Yes, sir?" Captain Bridget McCarthy answered.

"Put on a pair of gloves and help us for a few minutes, will you?"

"Can't, Hawk," Captain Bridget McCarthy said. "I've just got too much to do already."

"Then find somebody else."

"Yes, sir."

Ten minutes later, Hawkeye was aware of the help—gowned, capped, masked and gloved—at his left. Without looking up he reached over and put the new assistant's hands on a retractor.

"Pull," he said.

"How, Hawk?" he heard Father Mulcahy say. "This is a little out of my line."

For days, now, and for nights, too, Dago Red had been doing his part. All day and all night he had been going from patient to patient—black, white, yellow—friend and foe. Some of them didn't know who he was, but they all knew the side he was on. A confident patient does better in surgery, and so does a confident surgeon, and Dago Red had the right words for both.

"Just pull," Hawkeye was saying now. "Right there, and toward you. More. Good. And when we get out of this you can put in the first sterile fix in the history of surgery."

And still they came. Bellies, chests, necks, arteries, arms, legs, eyes, testicles, kidneys, spinal cords, all shot to hell.

Win or lose. Life and death. At the beginning of it, all of the surgeons, and particularly the Swampmen, had experienced a great transformation. During periods of only sporadic employment they often drank far too much and complained far too much, but with the coming of The Deluge they had become useful people again, a fulfilled, effective fighting unit and not just a bunch of semi-employed stew bums stranded in the middle of nowhere. This was fine, as far as it went, but it was going too far. By the end of the second week they were all wan, red-eyed, dog-tired and short of temper, and it was obvious to all of them that their reflexes had been dulled and that their judgment had sometimes become questionable.

"This can't go on," Lt. Col. Henry Blake was saying at five forty-five one afternoon, for the fiftieth or sixtieth time within the last three or four days. "Goddam it and to hell, but this just can't go on."

Henry was standing, with the Swampmen, just outside the door of the postop ward. Once again, somehow, they had managed to take care of all the major cases, and the debridements and fractures and amputations were now being handled by others. They had ostensibly stepped out for a smoke, but each knew that they were all there to post a watch to the north and hope against hope against the appearance of the six o'clock choppers.

"It's gotta end sometime," Henry was saying. "It's gotta end sometime."

"All actions and all wars," Trapper John said, "eventually do."

"Oh, hell, McIntyre," Henry said, "what good is that? When? That's the question. When?"

"I don't know," Trapper said.

"But who the hell does know?" Henry said. "I call three times a day, but those people in Seoul don't know a damn thing more than we do. Who the hell does know?"

111

"I don't know," Hawkeye said, "but maybe Radar . . ."

"O'Reilly, sir," Radar O'Reilly said, at the colonel's elbow.

"Goddam it, O'Reilly," Henry said, "don't do that!"

"Sir?"

"What the hell are you doing out here, anyway?"

"I thought you called for me, sir," Radar said.

"Look, O'Reilly . . . ," the colonel started to say.

"Look, Henry," Hawkeye said, "maybe I'm going off my nut . . ."

"Maybe we all are," Henry said.

"Then maybe Radar can help us."

"We *are* crazy," Henry said, shaking his head. "We're absolutely mad."

"Look, Radar," Hawkeye said. "What we . . ."

"Let me handle this, Pierce," Henry said. "O'Reilly?"

"Sir?"

"Now don't lie to me . . ."

"Why, sir! You know that I never . . ."

"Never mind that, O'Reilly," Henry said. "I don't want to listen to any of that, but I want to know something."

"What, sir?"

"Goddam it," Henry said, turning to the others. "I haven't really gone out of my mind, have I?"

"No you haven't, Henry," Trapper said. "Go ahead."

"Yeah, go ahead," Duke said.

"Look, O'Reilly," Henry said, looking right at Radar. "What do you hear?"

"Nothing, sir."

"Nothing!" Henry said. "What the hell do you mean, nothing?"

"I don't hear anything, sir."

"Well, what does that mean?"

"I believe it means, sir," Radar said, "that the action has subsided in the north."

"Good!" Duke said.

"Look, O'Reilly," Henry said. "Are you telling the truth?"

"Why, sir! You know that I never . . ."

"Stop that, O'Reilly!"

"Yes, sir."

"Radar," Hawkeye said. "Tell us something else."

"Yes, sir?"

"Do you hear the six o'clock choppers?"

"No, sir."

"You sure?"

"Yes, sir."

"Well, how the hell are you going to hear them, anyway, standing here?" Henry said, and he pointed toward the north. "You should be listening out there."

"Yes, sir," Radar said.

Radar started to walk slowly toward the north then, and they followed him. They formed a small procession, Radar in the lead, his ears at the right-angle red alert, his head turning on his long, thin neck in the familiar sweeping action. They walked across the bare ground the fifty yards to the barbed wire, beyond which lay the mine field, and they stopped.

"Well?" Henry said.

"Nothing, sir."

"Keep trying."

"Yes, sir."

To the north the valley was blanketed in shadow now, the hills to the left dark, but the sunset colors still bathing the tops of the hills to the east. They stood behind O'Reilly, where they could watch him and the sky at the same time, and they maintained absolute silence. As they watched, the last of the colors left the eastern hills, the dusk mounted in the valley and only the sky held light.

"O'Reilly," Henry said, "it's six o'clock."

"Nothing, sir."

"It's six-oh-five."

"Nothing, sir."

"O'Reilly," the colonel said, at about six-fifteen, "I can't see my watch any more."

"Nothing, sir."

"Glory be!" the Duke said.

"Good work, O'Reilly," the colonel said. "Dismissed."

"Thank you, sir."

"And by the way, Radar," Hawkeye said, "stop by The Swamp tomorrow for a bottle of Scotch."

"Thank you, sir," Radar said. "That's very kind of you, sir, but you were thinking of two."

"OK," said Hawkeye. "You're right, and you've got two."

"Thank you, sir."

"We're all crazy," Henry said.

There was no jubilation. They were all too tired. In fact, they were exhausted, completely spent, and the Swampmen hit their sacks. When 6:00 A.M. came and went, and there were no choppers, they slept on, and at 8:00 A.M., when Radar O'Reilly, accompanied by an associate lab technician, entered The Swamp, he could have made any of the three the victim of his desperate need, not for two fifths of Scotch, but for a pint of A-negative blood, quantities of which were on order from Seoul but had not arrived.

"Captain Forrest?" he said, shaking the Duke. "Sir?"

"Not now, honey," the Duke mumbled. "Gobacksleep."

Gently, Radar straightened Duke's right arm. Deftly, he injected Novocaine over a vein. Duke stirred but did not awaken, and while the assistant tightened the sleeve of Duke's T-shirt to serve as a tourniquet, Radar skillfully inserted a No. 17 needle into the vein and joyfully extracted a pint.

"Where'd you get it?" Colonel Blake asked, after Radar had hurriedly cross-matched it and proudly presented it to his chief. "Twenty minutes ago you said there wasn't any."

"I found a donor, sir," said Radar.

114

"Good boy," said the colonel.

Two hours later the colonel himself was a visitor to The Swamp. By now Hawkeye was in the middle of Muscongus Bay between Wreck Island and Franklin Light. He and his father, Big Benjy Pierce, were hauling lobster traps.

"Finest kind," Hawkeye was saying.

"C'mon, Pierce," Henry was saying, shaking him. "C'mon. Wake up!"

"What's wrong, Pop?"

"Pop, hell!" Henry said. "It's me."

"Who?" Hawkeye said.

"Listen, Pierce," Henry said. "There's a Korean kid in preop with a hot appendix. Who's going to take it out?"

"You are," Trapper John said, rolling over in his sack.

"Why me?" Henry said.

"Because," Trapper mumbled, "although you are a leader of men, there are no men left."

10

The business of doing major surgery on poor-risk patients can be trying and heartbreaking at any time, and when it is done regularly it can have an increasingly deleterious effect upon those who are doing it. It was therefore inevitable that The Deluge should have its after-effects, not only on the patients who survived but also on the surgeons who contributed to that survival. The first of the Swampmen to give outward evidence of what they had all been through was Hawkeye Pierce, and the first man to get caught in the fall-out was the anesthesiologist—Ugly John.

A good anesthesiologist is essential to any important surgical effort. Without one, the greatest surgeon in the world is helpless. With one, relatively untalented surgeons can look good. If the man at the head of the table understands the surgical problem and the surgeon's needs, if he understands the physiology and pharmacology of carrying a patient through a hazardous procedure, if he can have the patient under deep and controlled anesthesia when it is needed and

116

awake or nearly so at the end of the operation, he is an anesthesiologist and a boon to all mankind. If all he can do is keep the patient unconscious, he is just a gas-passer. There were more gas-passers than anesthesiologists in Korea, but in Captain Ugly John Black, limpid-eyed, dark-haired, and the handsomest man in the outfit, the 4077th had an anesthesiologist.

Ugly John probably worked harder than anyone else in the unit. Theoretically his responsibilities consisted only of supervising the anesthesia service. Actually, as the only one formally trained in anesthesiology, he was morally if not militarily bound to be available at all times. Too often this involved day after day of twenty-four hour duty, with only an occasional catnap. During busy periods like The Deluge the surgeons were constantly aware of his almost perpetual state of exhaustion and his greater than average effort. Nevertheless, when they had a tough one, they either wanted Ugly John to give the anesthesia or they wanted him to be around to check on it. Just his presence, or the knowledge that he was sacked out around the corner in the preop ward, was emotional balm to the man at the knife.

One of the most consistent customers of the 4077th MASH was the Commonwealth Division, consisting of British, Canadian, Australian, New Zealand and other assorted British Empire troops a few miles to the west. Captain Black had an intense, burning, complete, unremitting hatred for all the medical officers in the Commonwealth Division. His reason was very simple: they gave half a grain of morphine and a cup of tea to every wounded soldier. If the soldier was incapable of swallowing the tea, he still got the half grain of morphine. As a result of this treatment, it was frequently necessary to wait for the morphine to wear off before a patient's condition could be assessed. If early surgery seemed reasonable or mandatory, Ugly John, in the process of getting the patient to sleep, often caught the tea in his lap. Frequently the patient had holes in his stomach or small bowel. In this situation, Ugly did not catch the tea in his lap. The surgeon would aspirate it from the abdominal cavity where it had leaked through the holes. The surgeons of the 4077th had the largest series of tea peritonitis cases in recorded medical history.

When leisure came his way, Ugly's first duty was to repair his intratracheal tubes. These are tubes placed in a patient's windpipe through the mouth and attached to a machine, controlled by the anesthesiologist, which delivers oxygen and anesthetic agents in the concentrations desired. Inside the windpipe the tubes are held in place by small balloons which are inflated after their introduction.

The balloons on Ugly's intratracheal tubes, like all balloons, kept blowing out. The supply of new tubes was limited or nonexistent, for reasons never quite clear, so it was up to Captain Black to keep them in constant repair. There was only one source of new balloons.

Every week or ten days the PX received a shipment of the various things PX's receive shipments of. This always caused a line to form, and the line always included most of the nurses. At the head of the line, however, would be Ugly John Black. As the PX opened for business, Ugly John would step up and announce in a loud, clear, purposeful voice: "I'll take sixty rubber contraceptive devices. I hope to hell they're better than the last batch. They all leaked." Then he'd turn around and look austerely at the interested throng, few of whom knew what he did with sixty such items a week.

When not working or blending intratracheal tubes and contraceptives into efficient units, Ugly was known to have a drink or two. In these situations, he usually wound up in The Swamp and vented his spleen upon the entire medical profession of the British Empire.

"Those lousy bastards!" he would yell. "There isn't a god-damned one of them would shake hands with his grandmother. He'd rather knock her on her ass with half a grain of morphine and then drown her with a cup of tea."

Such a man was bound to be held in high esteem by the Swampmen and was considered a warm and welcome friend. Actually, the incident involving Hawkeye and Ugly John was a minor one—at least, as it concerned them—but it was the first sign of things to come.

In The Swamp, every problem case ever done at the 4077th was discussed, dissected and analyzed from every possible angle and in every conceivable detail. The Deluge had left much for discussion, and two nights after its end the Swampmen were thus engaged when the door opened and a corpsman stuck his head in.

"Hey, Hawkeye," he said, "they want you in the OR."

"I'm not on duty. Tell them to go fry their asses."

"The Colonel says to get your ass over there."

"OK."

Over in the OR, two of the night shift had the typical difficult war surgical problem with major wounds of chest, abdomen and extremities. The abdominal wounds alone made it a bad risk, and there was little margin for error. They needed help and advice. Hawkeye scrubbed up and was briefed by Ugly John.

"So how much blood," Hawkeye wanted to know, "did they give him before they started operating?"

"One pint," said Ugly.

"For Chrissake, John, why in hell do you let these cowboys start a case like this on one pint?"

"Well," Ugly started to say, "they . . ."

"Look, goddamit," Hawkeye went on. "You know as well as I do he should have had another hour and at least three pints before they brought him in here. What the hell's the matter with you, anyway?"

"I can't do everything around here," Ugly said. "I'm just the goddamned anesthesiologist."

"That doesn't stop you from thinking, does it?"

"The surgeons said he was ready," Ugly said. "These guys have been doing OK, so I haven't been arguing with them . . ."

"Then don't argue with me," Hawkeye said.

"So you're right," Ugly said, "but I'll tell you this. You're getting pretty hard to live with, Pierce."

"And that kid on the table may be pretty hard for someone to live without," Hawkeye said.

Then he got into the case and took it over. He concluded it as quickly as possible. He used every trick he'd learned in ten months of war surgery, and then he called in Dago Red to put in a fix.

"Please, Red," he said, "bring him in."

Too much is too much. Despite all efforts and fixes, the boy died an hour after surgery.

Father Mulcahy led Captain Pierce to Father Mulcahy's tent, gave him a cigarette and a canteen half full of Scotch and water. Lying on Red's sack, Hawkeye dragged on the butt, swallowed the drink and said, "Red, my curve's hanging, and I lost the hop on my fast ball."

"Speak English, Hawk. Maybe I can help you."

"Listen to Losing Preacher Mulcahy," Hawkeye said. "You'd like to get me snapping the mackerel, wouldn't you?"

"Oh, come off it, Hawk," Dago Red said. "You know me too well to say something like that."

"Yes, I do, Red. I'm sorry. I seem to be a little overextended these days, but I'll get over it. I can be a little nutty now and then, but I ain't a nut."

"I know you're not," Dago Red said, "but you people in The Swamp have got to get over the idea that you can save everyone who comes into this hospital. Man is mortal. The wounded can stand only so much, and the surgeon can do only so much."

"Red, that lousy can't-win-'em-all philosophy is no good.

120

In The Swamp the idea is that if they arrive here alive, they can leave alive if everything is done just right. Obviously this can't always be, but as an idea it's better than fair, so spare me all the rationalizations."

"Hit the sack, Hawk," Father Mulcahy said. "You still need sleep."

Hawkeye hit the sack, but the sleep he found was troubled and restless. At nine o'clock the next morning he entered the life and abdomen of Captain William Logan.

Captain William Logan, the still fairly youthful manager of a large supermarket, had joined the Mississippi National Guard soon after his release from five years of service in World War II. When the Misssissippi National Guard was summoned to Korea, Captain Logan had left the supermarket, his wife, his new set of Ben Hogan matched clubs and his three kids to go with them.

Captain Logan, Major Lee, who was an undertaker, and Colonel Slocum, who owned the Cadillac distributorship, were all from the same town. They belonged to the same Masonic Lodge and the same country club. Colonel Slocum, Major Lee and Captain Logan were very disturbed the morning the gooks lobbed one in on Captain Logan's 105mm howitzer battery, and Captain Logan's abdomen got in the way of a couple of shell fragments.

When Hawkeye Pierce operated on Captain Logan he had had enough sleep, and too much of everything else. He removed a foot of destroyed small bowel and re-anastomosed it, that is, reunited the ends of the remaining intestine. When done, he thought that the anastomosis might be too tight but he elected to leave it. That was a mistake, but only one of two.

For the next eight days Captain Logan did poorly. Each day he was worse. Hawkeye watched him, worried and worked, and every time he turned around he encountered

Colonel Slocum and Major Lee who wanted to know how things were going.

"Not too well," Hawkeye kept telling them.

"Why not?" they asked.

On the eighth day, they asked three times why things weren't going too well.

"Because, goddamn it, I did a lousy anastomosis," Hawkeye informed them.

On the ninth day, Hawkeye took Captain Logan, now desperately ill, back to the OR. He fixed the inadequate anastomosis, discovered at the same time that he had missed a hole in the rectum, did a colostomy, and five days later Captain Logan, much improved and out of danger, was evacuated. This was Saturday, and on Saturday night people from everywhere came to the tent which served as an Officers' Club for the 4077th.

Hawkeye Pierce, having learned a valuable lesson, having retrieved Captain Logan from the brink but still disgusted with himself, entered. Standing at the bar with a bottle of fine Scotch whiskey were Colonel Slocum and Major Lee, who beckoned to him.

Hawkeye's spirits plummeted even lower. His head hung. "The bastards are going to beat me up," he thought, "and they got a right to." He walked to the bar and joined them.

"Captain Pierce," Colonel Slocum said, handing him a drink, "there's something we want to tell y'all."

"I figured as much."

"We want to tell y'all that it makes us men up on the line feel mighty good to know that there are doctors like you around to take care of us if we get hurt."

Hawkeye was dumbfounded. He took a big pull on the Scotch and said, "For Christ sake, Colonel, don't you realize that I blew this one? I almost killed your buddy with bad surgery. I got him out of trouble, but he never shoulda been in it!"

122

"We been watchin' you, Pierce," Colonel Slocum said, with Major Lee at his side nodding assent. "Y'all worried about that man like he was your own brother, and he's OK now. That's all we need to know. We don't even care if you're a Yankee. Have another drink, Hawkeye!"

"Jeezus!" Hawkeye said. He put his glass down on the bar, turned his back on Colonel Slocum and Major Lee, and walked away from them and out the door.

It was three days later that Trapper John and the Duke caught the kid named Angelo Riccio, out of East Boston. Private Riccio didn't look too bad. He was alert. His pulse was a little rapid. His blood pressure was strong enough at one hundred over eighty. He had a variety of shell fragment wounds, only one of which seemed important.

Duke Forrest, coming in to work the night shift and drifting down the line of wounded, had been unimpressed by Angelo until he saw the X-ray. Angelo's heart looked too big. Examining the wounds again, Duke decided that one of the shell fragments could have hit the heart, causing hemorrhage into the pericardium, which surrounds and contains it.

Duke found Trapper John in the mess hall, watching a movie he had already seen twice in the States. Trapper came. He looked at the X-ray, and he and Duke sat down next to Angelo.

"How do you think the Sox'll make out this year?" Trapper asked the kid.

"Without the big guy they got nothin'," said Angelo, "and the big guy's over here somewhere."

"That's right," Trapper said. "Does that make you feel good, knowing that even a guy like that is over here?"

"Are you kiddin', Doc?" Angelo said. "I wouldn't wish this kind of thing on a dog. I'd feel much better if he was back over there bustin' up a few ball games for us."

"Well, he will be again," Trapper said, "and you'll be there to see him."

"Where you from, Doc?" Angelo asked.

"Winchester."

"You know my cousin, Tony Riccio? He's about your age."

"Sure I know him, Angelo. He caught for Winchester High."

"Yeah," Angelo said. "The Sox were interested in him, and then he threw out his arm."

Old Home Week ended.

"Angelo, we're going to operate on you," said Trapper.

"OK," Angelo said, "so operate on me. You're the Doc."

Trapper and Duke operated on him. Trapper lined it up ahead of time. "He's got blood in his pericardium. Before we open it we've got to have control of the vena cavae. We've got to have plenty of blood. Once we get to the heart we've got to close the holes quick or we lose."

They did it all as right as they could, but when they opened the pericardium everything went to hell. The shell fragment had made several small holes in the right atrium. Trapper and Duke handled it better than any other two people in Korea could have, but they and Angelo needed three or four more minutes.

Angelo died. He would never see Ted Williams step to the plate again, and half an hour later Dago Red found Trapper John McIntyre wandering around in the dark, took him to his tent and gave him a can of beer. Then he went in search of Duke Forrest and found him alone in The Swamp. The Duke had already opened a can of beer, but he wasn't drinking it. He was crying into it.

"And a Yankee, too," the Duke said, to cover his embarrassment when he looked up and saw Dago Red. "You know somethin'? The way I'm goin' I shouldn't even be operatin' on Yankees."

It was obvious that something had to be done for the Swampmen. It was obvious, of course, to Dago Red, and it was obvious to Colonel Blake who realized that he had a

124

serious problem on his hands—his problem boys were too exhausted and too dispirited to create their usual problems. It was also obvious to Radar O'Reilly who, tuned in as he was to everyone, was the most empathic member of the 4077th MASH, and who came up with two solutions.

The first of these was Dr. R. C. Carroll. Dr. R. C. Carroll had arrived at the Double Natural about five weeks before, was from deepest Oklahoma and somehow, while acquiring a medical education and two years of post-graduate training, had remained curiously unexposed to certain elements of human existence. Trapper John, most urbane of the Swampmen, had put the handle on Dr. Carroll.

"I thought I lived with the two biggest rubes in Korea," Trapper John said, "until this jeeter came along."

"Jeeter" became his name. Being new in the outfit he was not yet a member of the inner circle that gathered regularly at The Swamp for a drink before supper, but he did drop in occasionally. One afternoon, during the depth of the depression that followed The Deluge, he knocked on the door and was bade to enter. The Swampmen were alone.

"Excuse me," Jeeter said, "but Corporal O'Reilly said you fellas wanted to see me."

"Radar," said Hawkeye, who had been mooning into his martini, "must have his wavelengths mixed."

"Don't pay any attention to Captain Pierce," Trapper John said, handing Jeeter a water glass filled with a martini he had mixed for himself. "Sit down and have a drink."

"What is it?" Jeeter inquired.

"A martini, more or less," Trapper said.

"It looks like water," Jeeter said.

"That's right," Trapper said, "and it's sort of like water, but you don't drink it when you're thirsty."

"Right," the Duke said.

"Oh," Jeeter said.

Perhaps Jeeter was thirsty. He finished the drink in five

125

minutes and indicated his need for another. Trapper gave him another, although somewhat reluctantly.

"You know somethin'?" Jeeter said.

"What?" the Duke said.

"Ah only been here a little over a month," Jeeter said, "but ah'm hornier than a bitch in heat."

"Good," the Duke said.

"Yeah," Hawkeye said. "That just indicates you're healthy."

"Oh," Jeeter said.

"So what's your problem?" Hawkeye said.

"Well," Jeeter said, "what do ah do?"

"Did you ever think of the nurses?" Hawkeye said.

"All the time, but ah figured they were all took or didn't put out."

"I'll give you a word on nurses, Jeeter," volunteered Captain Pierce. "They're human, just like us."

"Oh," Jeeter said.

"Some of them do all of the time, some of them do some of the time, and observation over a period of many months convinces me that very few of them are queer."

"Oh," Jeeter said, halfway through his second martini now, "but how do ah go about it?"

"Don't ask me," said Trapper. "Captain Pierce, here, seems to be the big authority."

"Well," Hawkeye said, warming to the assignment, "there are two methods. One is the simple, staid, stateside, hackneyed, civilian approach where you devote all your spare time for a week, softening the broad up with drinks, eating with her, taking her to Seoul on her day off, to our so-called Officers' Club on Saturday night, getting her stoned and then escorting her to a tent or down to the river with a blanket."

"Oh," Jeeter said.

"But if you go with the blanket," Hawkeye said, "under no circumstances should you proceed more than ten yards north from the O Club because you might place the blanket

126

on top of a mine. An exploding mine may give the protagonist and his partner the impression that he's Thor, the God of Thunder, but actually it's the worst form of coitus interruptus."

"Right," the Duke said.

"And, of course," Hawkeye said, "this method doesn't guarantee success. You may strike out. The flower of femininity you select may require not one but two weeks of cultivation, and then you run into the law of diminishing returns. Our leading tacticians recommend a week at the outside for this method."

"Oh," Jeeter said, indicating a desire for martini number three, "but what's the second method?"

"The second method is quicker and statistically almost as sound. You talk to the broad for a few minutes in some social situation, preferably over a drink, and you say, 'Honey, let's go somewhere and tear off a piece.' Either she says OK, or she takes off like a candy-assed baboon. The big plus of this method is that you either score fast or lose fast, and if you lose you can go on to the next blossom without further waste of time, effort and good booze."

"But which do you recommend?" asked Jeeter.

"Well, I don't really know," said Hawkeye. "This is mostly theory with me. What do you think, Trapper?"

"Well," Trapper said, "maybe he should announce his availability. Most of them will be in the mess hall swilling coffee, so let's go eat."

Jeeter, by now finding even ambulation a difficult exercise, was assisted to the door of the mess hall. Most of the nurses were indeed present, and Jeeter, silhouetted in the doorway but with the Swampmen out of sight on either side of him, made his announcement.

"Ah'm gonna screw every goddam nurse in the place!" he proclaimed loudly.

127

"Starting with Hot-Lips Houlihan," Trapper John whispered to him.

"Startin' with Hot-Lips Houlihan!" Jeeter shouted.

The Swampmen did not follow him in. They went back to The Swamp, had a short one and ate later. The next morning Jeeter knew only that he felt terrible and, after Colonel Blake had chewed him out, that he was in disgrace. It remained for Roger the Dodger Danforth, in a matter of hours, to take him off the hook.

Roger the Dodger Danforth was a surgeon at the 6073rd MASH, twenty-five miles to the East. Roger and Ugly John Black had trained together in the States, so Roger and the Swampmen were all well acquainted. In fact, they shared a mutual disrespect for most things held dear by others and a mutual respect for each other, and although Roger the Dodger was not considered, by observers of both phenomena, to be a greater menace than the three members of The Swamp, he was held to be at least their equal.

"Thank God," Colonel Blake would say, after Roger the Dodger's visits, "that that sonofabitch isn't assigned here, too."

On the day following Jeeter's pronunciamento in the portal of the mess hall, Roger the Dodger arrived about noon. Hawkeye had just finished amputating the leg of the only customer of the morning—a Korean who had thought himself immune to minefields—and he had gone to the mess tent for a light lunch.

"Where are the boys?" he asked Dago Red.

"Roger the Dodger is here," Dago Red said. "He and Ugly and your boys are over in The Swamp, and may the Lord have mercy on us all."

"Second the motion," Hawkeye said, "and I better have a large lunch."

After the large lunch, Hawkeye headed for The Swamp with an equal mixture of anticipation and reluctance. Halfway across the ball field that separated The Swamp from the mess tent he was greeted by Roger the Dodger, who stood in the doorway of The Swamp with a glass in his hand and yelled: "Hi, Hawkeye, you old shitkicker! Screw the Regular Army! How they goin'?"

"Finest kind," Hawkeye said.

"Have a drink," Roger the Dodger invited. "Brung two bottles of my own."

"What the hell are you doing here, anyway?" Hawkeye wanted to know.

"I don't know," Roger the Dodger said. "All I know is, last night I had a call from some goddam Colonel O'Reilly who said to come . . ."

"Who?" Hawkeye said.

"I don't know," Roger the Dodger said. "The only O'Reilly you got in this outfit is some corporal looks like a goddamn weathervane. What difference does it make? Have a drink."

"I just might," Hawkeye said.

They all had several, and a glow of amiable incandescence began to suffuse The Swamp. All might have gone well, except that Roger the Dodger, apparently the recipient of a call to take this light out into the world, insisted on stepping to the door every fifteen minutes to yell: "Screw the Regular Army!"

Daily at 3:00 P.M., and for an hour, the showers at the 4077th MASH were reserved for the nurses. The nurses, some past the first bloom of youth, some not on diets, had to pass The Swamp en route to and from their ablutions, and it was a portion of this processional that crossed the field of vision of Roger the Dodger on one of his trips outdoors to exhort the populace to violation.

"All the nurses," Roger the Dodger yelled now, "are elephants!"

Then he switched the call to: "All the elephants have clap!"

"And Hot-Lips Houlihan," Trapper John suggested, "is the head mahout, and must be held responsible."

"And Hot-Lips Houlihan," Roger the Dodger yelled, "is the head mahout, and must be held responsible!"

That had the expected result. For the past two hours Colonel Henry Blake had been sitting in his tent listening to the exhortations and hoping against hope. He had called in Father John Patrick Mulcahy and, over beers, they had discussed possibilities.

"Frankly," Colonel Blake had said, "I'm scared. Any commanding officer with half a brain wouldn't let this go on."

"I disagree with you, Colonel," Father Mulcahy had said. "Something had to break, and I was afraid it was going to be our friends over there."

"I know," the Colonel said. "The other day that Duke called me 'sir.' At any moment I've been expecting Hawkeye Pierce to salute me. They're not well, I tell you. They've been pressed too hard, and that's why I let that Roger the Dodger in there again. Something's got to happen."

"And it's about to," Father Mulcahy said as the two, aghast, heard Roger the Dodger invoke the name of the Chief Nurse. "I think I'll go over to my place, or would you rather I stay?"

"No," Colonel Blake said. "It's all my fault, so I'll handle this Amazon alone."

Father Mulcahy had no sooner departed than Major Margaret Houlihan arrived. She arrived right from the showers, the ends of her hair still wet and the strap of her shower cap trailing from one end of her rolled towel. She was irate, and try as he might, Henry could not tune her out.

"This isn't a hospital," he heard his Chief Nurse screaming at him. "It's an insane asylum, and you're to blame . . ."

"Now, just a minute, Major," Henry started to say. "You . . ."

"Don't you minute-major me," his Chief Nurse went on.

"If you don't stop those beasts, those THINGS, that one they call Trapper John from addressing me as Hot-Lips and stirring up those others, I'm going to resign my commission and . . ."

"Oh, goddammit, Hot-Lips," Henry heard himself saying, "resign your goddamn commission, and get the hell out of here!"

Five minutes later, Radar O'Reilly was awakened from a sound sleep. He was awakened by a telephone conversation between Major Houlihan and General Hammond, in which Major Houlihan was pouring out a lively story of a military hospital with everything out of control. This was followed by a conversation between General Hammond and Colonel Blake, in which Radar heard General Hammond say: "Henry, for Christ's sake, what the hell's going on up there? You get down here tomorrow morning at 0930, and your story better be a goddamn good one."

Radar hastened to The Swamp. By now Roger the Dodger, having added another chapter to his legend, had departed for his hospital, leaving the Swampmen and Ugly John to clean up the carnage. Radar filled them in on what he had heard.

"You know, Henry might really be in trouble," Hawkeye said, after Radar had finished his report and left. "That damn fool nurse has finally become a real menace."

"That's right," the Duke said.

"Trapper," Hawkeye said, "why do you always have to call her 'Hot-Lips'?"

"I don't always have to call her 'Hot-Lips.' This morning I was nice to her. I called her 'Major Hot-Lips'."

"What'll we do?" asked the Duke.

"Well," Trapper said, "I guess that if I hadn't called that bomber 'Hot-Lips' and then treed her with Jeeter and Roger the Dodger, the General wouldn't be on Henry's ass. Therefore, I'll go down and square it with the General."

131

"We'll go with you!" chorused Forrest and Pierce.

They made an appointment with the General for nine o'clock the next morning but appeared in his outer office at eight-thirty. They were wearing fatigues that had that lived-in look, without insignia, and they sat down on the bench that ran along one wall. Three quite attractive members of the Women's Army Corps—a lieutenant and two sergeants—occupied the working space of this outer part of the General's sanctum.

"Well," Trapper John said, after a few minutes, "shall we?"

"Why not?" Hawkeye Pierce said.

Each of the Swampmen produced from the recesses of his clothing a bottle labeled Johnny Walker Black Label. Earlier, back at the Double Natural, these bottles had been filled with tea by Sergeant Mother Divine, and now Duke Forrest rose from the bench and approached the WAC lieutenant.

"Y'all got any paper cups, honey?" he asked politely.

Confused, the lieutenant produced paper cups. The cups were filled, and cigarettes were lighted.

"Think the broads might like some tea?" wondered Trapper John in a stage whisper.

"They ain't broads," answered Hawkeye. "They're two sergeants and a lieutenant."

"Which are higher, sergeants or captains?" inquired the Duke. "Do we outrank them?"

"I dunno," said Trapper.

"Even if they outrank us, they might like some tea," said Hawkeye.

Duke rose again, the compleat southern gentleman.

"Pardon, ladies, but would y'all care for some tea?"

"No, thank you," the lieutenant answered frostily.

The Swampmen sipped their tea in silence. Suddenly, the silence was shattered by Trapper John: "I bet generals get plenty."

The lieutenant shot from behind her desk.

"Who are you people?" she demanded in great indignation.

"Don't get overheated, honey," Hawkeye said. "We're just a bunch of screwups from up the line. We gotta see the General at nine o'clock, civilian time, to chew him out."

"The General is supposed to see three medical officers at nine o'clock," she snapped, regaining a trace of composure.

"That's us, ma'am," spoke up Duke Forrest. "If you ladies don't happen to feel well, we'd admire to give y'all an examination."

Despite the rigid training required to reach officer and upper enlisted rank in the WAC, the lieutenant and her troops were totally unprepared for this sort of situation. They deserted in the face of the enemy.

"Must be a coffee break," observed Hawkeye.

After a few minutes of idle chatter, the Swampmen found time hanging heavy. Hawkeye produced a pair of dice and a crap game started.

At eight fifty-nine General Hammond arrived. As he walked through the outer sanctum toward his inner sanctum he was annoyed to find his secretarial force gone, and the spectacle of three disheveled crapshooters and three bottles of Johnny Walker Black Label annoyed him even more.

"Hiya, General, how they goin'?" Hawkeye inquired.

The General stood transfixed.

"The Duke's trying to make a four," Trapper John informed the General.

"Little Joe," Duke begged the dice.

"Duke can't make fours," Hawkeye assured the General. "He'll crap out in a minute and we'll be with you."

Duke sevened and stood up. "Nice to see y'all, General," he said. "Y'all sure got it knocked—three nice lookin' WAC's workin' for y'all, and comin' to work in the middle of the mornin'."

"We got here early," Trapper John explained, "because we spent the night in a whore house, and we had to get out before the day shift took over. Have a shot of tea?"

He offered his bottle to the General. The General remained transfixed.

"Come in," he finally commanded. Followed by the Swampmen, the General stalked into his office. Safely behind his desk, the General scowled at them.

"I've heard about you people," he said, "but I didn't really believe it. Now I do."

"You got some nice looking stuff working in your office, General," Hawkeye said.

"Shut up!" roared the General.

"General," Trapper said, "I'd like to change the tenor of this interview and be very serious. We've been in every hospital you have. The 4077th is the best you've ever had, and the biggest reason is Colonel Henry Braymore Blake. It was me that got that dizzy nurse mad when Henry had already had more than any of us needed. Do anything you want with us, but you'd be a damn fool to get rid of your best MASH commander because Hot-Lips Houlihan doesn't like her name."

The General grunted, took a nervous sip of water and lit a cigarette.

"Do you men really mean it?"

"General," said Hawkeye, "we know what we're talking about. We've seen more of the inside of these places than you have. We wouldn't be going out of our way for a Christless Regular Army Colonel if we didn't mean it! Begging your pardon, of course, General. I forgot."

"I'll bet," said the General, thinking hard now. "Suppose I replaced Henry with someone else? What would happen?"

"The guy'd never last," Trapper John informed him.

"Positively not," Hawkeye said.

"Right," the Duke said.

134

"OK," said the General. "I appreciate your coming. Don't worry about Henry."

The Swampmen scurried out one door, just before a harassed, scared and premature Henry, seemingly hurrying to his own execution, burst through another.

"Glad to see you, Henry," the General greeted him. "I probably shouldn't have made you come all the way down here. Fact is, I'm bored with the company around here. I wanted someone to have a couple of drinks and some lunch with."

"But what about Major Houlihan?" gulped Henry.

"You mean Hot-Lips?" asked the General. "Screw her."

"N-n-no th-thanks, G-General," replied Henry.

11 The temperature at noon, day after day, was between 95° and 100°. The temperature at midnight, night after night, was between 90° and 95°. As the tempo of the war picked up again, the wounded soldiers kept coming by ambulance and helicopter, and the Double Natural was too busy and too hot.

Surgery in the steaming heat beneath the tin roof of the Quonset hut was hard on the surgeons and not good for the patients. Both lost fluids and electrolytes. Captain Ugly John Black, the anesthesiologist, claimed that after any long case the patient, who'd been receiving the appropriate intravenous fluids, was usually healthier than the surgeon. Sleep for the weary workers was absolutely necessary but nearly impossible, particularly for the Swampmen, who were working the night shift and trying to sleep during the day. They gave up any idea of sleeping in The Swamp. Instead they went to the river a few hundred yards north, launched air mattresses, and slept half submerged, in the shade of the railroad bridge where the gentle current kept them wedged against the pilings.

Then two things happened. First, the fighting and therefore the surgery slacked off. Second, Colonel Henry Blake was sent to Japan for temporary duty at the Tokyo Army Hospital and replaced for the three weeks by Colonel Horace DeLong, another Regular Army doctor whose permanent assignment was at the Tokyo Army Hospital.

The period of hard work and the heat had put tempers on edge. About midnight, soon after Colonel DeLong arrived, a soldier was brought in with shell fragment wounds involving his belly and chest. The chest wounds weren't major but still required that a drainage tube be inserted in the chest for re-expansion of the lung. The abdominal wounds were major, but routine for the organization—the kind of case demanding a sensible plan of preoperative preparation, well controlled anesthesia, reasonably rapid, technically careful surgery, and an awareness, as Captain Hawkeye Pierce had learned again in the case of Captain William Logan, of how easy it is to miss one little hole in the bowel when there are ten or twelve.

Hawkeye Pierce was the gunner again in this one. He saw the X-rays, looked at the patient, knew what had to be done and when would be the best time to do it. He and Ugly John figured this would be about 3:00 A.M., after the patient had had some blood, after the closed thoracotomy had had its effect, and after the patient's pulse and blood pressure had stabilized.

By one-thirty there were indications that the patient was coming around and that 3:00 A.M. was a fairly shrewd call. At one-thirty, Hawkeye Pierce stepped into the Painless Polish Poker and Dental Clinic to pass the time until the knife dropped. At one-forty-five Colonel DeLong entered the Clinic and carried on as became his rank.

"Captain Pierce," he stated, "you have a seriously wounded

patient for whom you are responsible. I find you in a poker game."

Hawkeye knew the Colonel had years and overall experience on him, but he also knew that few people had the reflexes for this kind of surgery unless they'd been doing it day in and day out for a while. He understood the Colonel's unhappiness but, choosing to be unpleasant and uncooperative, he answered, "You betcher ass, Dad."

"What?" said the Colonel.

"Gimme three," said Hawkeye to Captain Waldowski.

The Painless Pole gave him three.

"Pierce," yelled Colonel DeLong, "the soldier requires emergency surgery."

"You betcher ass, Colonel."

"Well, Captain, are you going to take care of your patient, or are you going to play poker?"

"I'm going to play poker until 3:00 A.M. or until the patient is adequately prepared for surgery. However, if you'd like to operate on him yourself right now, be my guest, Colonel. I get the same pay whether I work or not."

The Colonel just stood there. Hawkeye held a pair of aces, didn't draw anything worth while, waited till the bet came to him and dropped out, knowing by then that the Painless Pole had filled either a straight or a flush.

The Colonel still stood there. Hawkeye lit a cigarette and ignored him. The Colonel said, "Pierce, I want to talk to you."

Hawkeye said, "Look, DeLong, my mood and my tenure of office in this organization add up to I don't want to talk to you. As far as I'm concerned, you're just another Regular Army croaker, and you all give me the red ass except maybe Henry Blake. Why don't you either take the case yourself or join me at three o'clock?"

Ignored by the poker players who were more interested in the game than in the side show, Colonel DeLong retreated. At two-forty-five Hawkeye left the game. The patient was

138

taken into the operating area. Ugly John started putting him to sleep.

"Send for Colonel DeLong," Hawkeye told a corpsman.

The Colonel arrived and joined Hawkeye at the scrub sink. Hawkeye was beginning to feel a little contrite.

"Colonel," he said, "at one-thirty this guy had had less than a pint of blood, and he'd lost two or three. His pulse then was 120, and his blood pressure was about 90. Now, at three o'clock, he's had three pints of blood. His pulse is 80 and his blood pressure 120. His collapsed lung is expanded. He's had a gram of Terramycin intravenously. We can operate on him safely. We should do it quickly, but we don't have to do it frantically or carelessly."

The operation went the usual route. Numerous holes had to be repaired, and one piece of small bowel had to be removed. After an hour all the apparent damage had been corrected.

"Now, Colonel," said Hawkeye, "I'm going to sandbag you. Do you figure we're ready to get out of this belly?"

"Obviously you don't think so, and I don't know why," admitted Colonel DeLong.

"Well, Dad, we haven't found any holes in the large bowel. They've all been in the small bowel, but the smell is different. I caught a whiff of large bowel, but it ain't staring us in the face, right?"

"Right," the Colonel said.

"So if it ain't staring us in the face it's got to be retroperitoneal," Hawkeye said, meaning that the perforation had to be in a portion of the large intestine hidden in the abdominal cavity. "Therefore, and from the look of the wounds, I figure he's got a hole in his sigmoid colon that we won't find unless we look for it."

They looked for it and found it. The Colonel was impressed. They closed the hole, did a colostomy and closed the belly.

139

Afterwards, over a cup of coffee, the Colonel said, "OK, Pierce, that was a nice job, but you must realize that I can't afford to tolerate the rudeness and insubordination you demonstrated when I tried to talk to you during the poker game."

"So don't afford it," suggested Hawkeye.

"Pierce, you don't like me, do you?"

"For Christ's sake, Colonel," exploded Hawkeye, "why don't you go to bed? Right now I don't even like myself, and all I need to set me off is to be bugged by a Regular Army medical officer."

The Colonel went to bed. There wasn't much else he could do.

Two days later there was no work at all. The heat persisted. It was too hot to drink. It was too hot to sleep. It was too hot to play baseball. It was too hot to play poker. The Swampmen made a halfhearted effort at rehabilitation. They'd been reading some Somerset Maugham stories about Malayan rubber plantations. At 9:00 A.M. they got their ice cube tray out of the refrigerator in the laboratory. Soon they were sitting in chairs in front of The Swamp holding tall glasses of Pimm's #1 Punch and making believe they were Malayan rubber plantation foremen. Whenever a Korean houseboy came into sight, they yelled at him to get to work and start turning out the rubber, and they were thus laconically passing the time when Colonel DeLong sauntered by.

"Good morning, gentlemen," he greeted them.

"You just out from home?" asked Trapper John.

"No, I've been in Tokyo for some time."

"Y'all married?" asked the Duke.

"Yes."

"Bring your wife with you?" asked Hawkeye.

"Of course not."

"I say, I wish I knew how you fellows get away with it," said Trapper. "We three have our brides along, and it's pure grief. They can't stand the beastly climate, and they won't

140

let us commingle with the native girls. You don't know how lucky you are!"

"I believe I'll wander down to the pool for a dip," said Hawkeye. He got his air mattress from the tent and headed for the river. The others followed, leaving the Colonel standing with his mouth open.

"Oh, I say, Colonel," Trapper called back to him, "perhaps you'd join us for a set or two of doubles later, after the heat has abated?"

So they went to the river, swam a little and slept a little. By 3:00 P.M., Hawkeye Pierce was awake, pensive and bored. He lay belly down and naked on his air mattress, peering into the murky water below.

"Hey, Duke," he asked, "whadda ya know about mermaids?"

"Nothin'," Duke assured him.

Trapper John, a leading authority on many subjects, joined the conversation. "In my opinion, there are mermaids in this river."

"I'm forced to keep an open mind on that," said Hawkeye. "Certainly if there are mermaids in this river, we'd be just plain foolish not to grab a few of them."

"How y'all gonna catch a mermaid?" asked Duke.

"In a mermaid trap, naturally," said the Hawk.

"How do you make a mermaid trap?"

"Just like a lobster trap, only bigger."

"Let's get goin' on it."

"OK."

They paddled ashore, dressed, went to the supply tent, where a cooperative sergeant provided material and tools. Hawkeye Pierce, in his boyhood, had built many lobster pots. For a man of his experience and background, the construction of a mermaid trap didn't seem to present a major problem, and the next morning found the Swampmen well along on their project when again Colonel DeLong dropped by.

"What are you doing here, gentlemen?" he asked.

"Buildin' us a mermaid trap," Duke informed him. "Y'all want to help?"

The Colonel was trying to blend into the environment. "I see," he said. "Where do you expect to catch mermaids?"

"The river's alive with them," answered Trapper.

"I see," said the Colonel again. "Assuming that you are able to catch one of these creatures, what do you propose to do with it?"

Hawkeye gave the Colonel a look of impatience and scorn. "We're gonna screw the ass off her," he stated.

The Colonel was desperately trying to hang in there. "Do you have reason to believe that mermaids may be effectively utilized for that purpose?"

"Oh, Finest Kind," Hawkeye assured him.

"Numero Uno," said Trapper John.

"Yeah," said the Duke.

Colonel DeLong retreated to his tent to think. Colonel Blake, before departing for Tokyo, had deliberately and perhaps maliciously not briefed him on the Swampmen.

Meanwhile, Hawkeye had words with the Duke and Trapper John, which went something like this: "I haven't built a lobster trap in years, and I've lost the touch. This mermaid trap has already become bigger than I am. Let's change the game. We got this guy DeLong buzzing anyhow. Let's convince him we're nuts, and maybe he'll ship us out for awhile until Henry gets back and catches on. They got psychiatrists in Seoul, and we'll be close enough to get back if business picks up."

Trapper took the cue. He went to the next tent and spoke to Rafael Rodriguez, a lieutenant in the Medical Service Corps.

"Rafe," he said, "we'd like a little help. Would you be willing to go tell Colonel DeLong we've flipped and suggest emergency psychiatric care?"

142

Rafael Rodriguez had been on The Swamp's list of non-surgical good boys for several months, and now he justified the faith bestowed upon him. He went to Colonel DeLong's tent, knocked respectfully and was bade to enter.

"Sit down. Have a beer, Lieutenant," the Colonel urged him.

"Thank you, Sir. Sir, you look troubled. Perhaps I could be of help. I've been here for some time, you know."

"Perhaps you could, Rodriguez," the Colonel said. "I'm new. This is a strange and unusual situation for me. I'm very worried about three of our surgeons: Pierce, McIntyre and Forrest. Their work, in the little time I've been here, has impressed me, but the last day or two their general behavior has caused me considerable concern."

"Sir, I don't blame you. In fact, that's why I've come to see you. I've known them since they came. They have been good men, but I'm compelled to say that I'm disturbed about them. Sir, I know them intimately. Something has happened. Sir, I think they need psychiatric care."

"That's all I need to hear," said Colonel DeLong. "I thought so, but I needed the confirmation of a reliable observer who's been on the scene longer than I. I'll take the responsibility of telling them about it."

"Thank you, Sir," said Rafael Rodriguez. "I don't think I'd be able to do it."

"I understand, Lieutenant," said Colonel DeLong.

Rafe took a back route to The Swamp, poured a Scotch and gleefully informed the occupants that they were to undergo psychiatric evaluation. He left after one Scotch, lest the Colonel catch him there. Half an hour later, Colonel DeLong entered The Swamp.

"Gentlemen," he said, "I'll come directly to the point. I am informed that your work here has been of exceptional quality. However, my own observations, confirmed by others, indicate that now you need help. Apparently prolonged responsibility in this situation, along with the heat and the isolation, has taken its toll. I've arranged for you to go to the 325th Evac tomorrow for a few days rest and to be seen by the psychiatric service. They will determine what happens next."

Hawkeye Pierce looked at Trapper John. "I always knew you was foolish," he said.

Duke Forrest whined, "I cain't go to no hospital. I gotta get me a mermaid."

Trapper John rose from his sack. "Colonel, if I could catch a mermaid tonight, you'd let me take her to the hospital with me, wouldn't you?"

"Of course!" said the Colonel.

"Colonel," said Hawkeye, "I'll go along with this for only one reason. A few days down there will give me a shot at the epileptic whore, which has become one of my life's ambitions, and in this general geographical location that's the only thing that interests me more than a mermaid."

Colonel DeLong desperately, all of a sudden, wanted to ask about the epileptic whore but restrained himself. "Transportation has been arranged," he told them. "You'll be picked up at 0800 hours."

"Finest Kind," agreed Hawkeye, as the Colonel left.

Duke and Trapper turned to Hawkeye.

"What's this about an epileptic whore?" they demanded.

"It just popped into my head. I got a buddy back home who's a psychiatrist. He had a patient who was an epileptic, and every time her husband tried her she threw a fit. All the guy had to do was plug himself in and the world went crazy. To me it always sounded like a great bit. For all I know, they may have an epileptic whore in Seoul. Anyway we might be able to use the idea. How do we handle the psychiatrist?"

Trapper was thinking, which was vaguely recognized by

144

his colleagues, so silence ensued for several minutes. Finally he spoke.

"We tell the headshrinker nothing except name, rank, serial number, and we want to get fixed up with the epileptic whore."

Silence again, while Duke and Hawkeye mulled it over.

"Whadda you think?" asked Trapper.

"I think Henry'll be back in four days," said Duke, "and that's how long we'll get away with this crap."

"I think it's OK," said Hawkeye. "Let's tell the shrink the broad's at Mrs. Lee's. I don't figure to spend four days down there without some psycho-sexual-physiological relief."

"I believe," said Trapper John, "that the group is in full accord in that area."

Trapper mixed another round of drinks. A few moments passed before Hawkeye spoke again.

"I figure we'd better think this over a little more," he said. "Psychiatrists are never overly troubled with the smarts, but even the dumbest one is going to smell a rat if we all go in and say the same thing. I kind of have a yen for this deal. Why don't you guys tell the shrink that you're OK, that you've been riding along to protect me, and that I've suddenly become much worse. I think I can drive whatever simple son-of-a-bitch we encounter out of his mind."

"I guess you're right, Hawk," Trapper agreed. "You got the ball."

"How y'all figure to handle it?" asked Duke.

"Easy," said the Hawk. "I'll talk gibberish to him. All you guys got to do is be very serious, impress him with your virtue, and emphasize that I've been effective and valuable until now, and you love me dearly. After an interview with him I'll meet you at Mrs. Lee's."

As Colonel DeLong had promised, the transportation arrived at 8:00 A.M., and the nuts were taken to the psychiatric section of the 325th Evacuation Hospital in Yong-Dong-Po.

Duke and Trapper walked in, solicitously leading Hawkeye. They were to see Major Haskell, the Chief of Psychiatry. Fortunately he had only been in Korea for two weeks, and news of the 4077th MASH had not reached him.

Trapper and Duke arranged to meet him first, explained that they had gone along with the mermaid gag in the hope of straightening Captain Pierce out, and that they had submitted to this ordeal themselves in the hope that he would snap out of it at the last moment. However, it was clear, just from his behavior in the last twelve hours, that Pierce's sanity had deteriorated alarmingly. They hoped that the Major would do everything possible to see that proper treatment was obtained without delay.

"We've been close to this man, Major," said Duke. "He's been a dedicated surgeon. He's been a tower of strength to us. Now he needs help. We know you'll do your best."

"I appreciate your help, gentlemen," Major Haskell assured them, "and I have some idea of how close the three of you have been. I understand the emotional involvement that men in your situation develop with one another. However, I can tell from the way you've presented this story that you have a grasp of the problem. I think you realize, and if you don't I must warn you, that this is a serious problem. It sounds to me like some form of schizophrenia, and in this sort of case, with the sudden deterioration you've described, the prognosis is usually not good."

"Oh," the Duke said.

"By the way," the Major continued, "I have Colonel DeLong's report here. He mentions something about an epileptic whore. What's that all about?"

"They got one at Mrs. Lee's," Trapper told him. "I hear she's real wild. We'll appreciate whatever you can do for Captain Pierce."

Duke and Trapper left, and Hawkeye was led in. The Major invited him to sit down and offered him a cigarette.

146

"How do you feel today, Captain?"

"I have sounded forth the trumpet that shall never call retreat. I am lifting out the hearts of men. Hey, you got any Harry James records?"

Major Haskell took a deep breath and ignored Captain Pierce's question.

"Tell me about yourself, Captain. Who are you?"

"Hawkeye Pierce."

"I know, but beyond that, what are you?"

"I'm the world's greatest short putter, to say nothing of being a descendant of Robert Ford."

"Who was he?"

"The dirty little coward who shot Mr. Howard."

"Why have you come down to see me today?"

"I ain't come down to see you. I came for the action."

"Do you mean the epileptic whore?"

"You betcher ever-lovin' A, Major."

"Captain, we're getting away from our subject. Something seems to have happened to you since Colonel DeLong took over your hospital."

"That's right, Sir. He's against me."

"What makes you think so?"

"The dirty mudder was gonna steal my mermaid."

"Is there anything else about Colonel DeLong that bothers you?"

"Yeah. He reminds me of my old man."

"I see," said Major Haskell. "Now perhaps we are getting somewhere. In what way does he remind you of your father?"

"He doesn't play tennis."

"Why doesn't your father play tennis?" Major Haskell asked, sort of by reflex, and regretted the question even before the answer.

"Because the harpies of the shore have plucked the eagle of the sea," Hawkeye explained. "He can't take the ball on the rise no more. They have laid poor Jesse in his grave."

147

"I see," answered the Major. "Captain Pierce, tell me about yourself. Feel free to talk. I want to help you. Perhaps if you'd just relax and open up and let the words come, you'd feel better and I'd be able to help you."

"Dad, I feel great."

"Talk to me anyhow, Captain. Just talk about anything that comes into your head."

"Death is an elephant, torch-eyed and horrible, foam-flanked and terrible," Hawkeye commented.

Major Haskell lit a cigarette.

"You nervous or something?" asked Hawkeye.

"Not at all," the Major replied, nervously.

"Hey, Dad, I'll give you a nice buy on an elephant. Velly clean. Takes penicillim. Finest kind."

"Captain Pierce, what are you up to? Frankly, I can't decide whether you're crazy or just some kind of a screwball."

"Well, why don't you mull it over for a while. You got anything to trade in?"

"What do you mean?"

"I mean you want a clean deal on a clean elephant, or you got some kind of used up elephant you wanta stick me with in return for my best elephant?"

"Look, Captain Pierce—"

"You hate me, don't you?" said Hawkeye. "Just like Duke and Trapper hate me."

"I'm sure no one hates you, Captain."

"They sure as hell do."

"Why?"

"Because I'm a great mahout. I'm an elephant boy. That's all I ever wanted to be but because the elephants like me so good, the people all hate me."

"Captain Pierce, I think we'll send you to the States for treatment."

"Finest Kind," said Hawkeye, rising, and added: "Be swift my soul to answer him, be jubilant my feet," and cut out on

148

swift, jubilant feet for Mrs. Lee's where he found Duke and Trapper John at lunch, or rather at pre-lunch martinis. They appeared unusually happy.

"Here's the nut," said Trapper. "How do they handle you hopelessly deteriorated schizophrenics nowadays?"

"The shrinker said he was gonna send me back to the States," Hawkeye informed them. "Maybe I oughta take him up on it. I don't know how they treat it, and I don't plan to find out. Now tell me why you guys look so happy."

"You'll never believe it, Hawk," Trapper filled him in, "but Mrs. Lee actually has an epileptic whore, or at least a babe who has some kind of convulsion every time she entertains a client. She's been scaring the customers silly, but with proper publicity she should go good."

Duke and Trapper had already told Mrs. Lee of the potential value of her convulsing employee. They had predicted that there would be some phone calls before long, inquiring as to her existence and availability. When the phone rang, it was answered by Mrs. Lee, whose round cherubic face broke into a wide smile as she nodded her head rapidly.

"Epileptic whore hava yes," she assured the party on the other end of the phone. "Velly clean, school teacher."

Mrs. Lee described all her girls as "velly clean." Beyond that, they were divided into three subcategories: movie actresses, cherry girls and school teachers. A girl's status varied with Mrs. Lee's usually shrewd estimate of the customer's needs.

There was a commotion at the front entrance as Major Haskell appeared with two M.P.'s. Hawkeye was led to an area of seclusion by Mrs. Lee as Major Haskell and his troops entered the dining room.

"Has Captain Pierce been here?" he demanded of Trapper and Duke.

"Hell, no," said Duke. "We figured you all had him under wraps. How'd he get away?"

149

"I don't know," said Haskell, "but that boy is way out. It's imperative that I find him."

"If I were you, I'd search the waterfront," suggested Trapper. "He might be looking for mermaids."

"How about you fellows helping out? You said he meant everything to you. I should think you'd help me find him before he harms himself or someone else."

"If he's all that crazy, the hell with him," said Trapper.

"Yeah," the Duke said. "We got appointments with the epileptic whore anyway."

"I'm tired of hearing about the epileptic whore," stated the Major. "What's it all about anyhow?"

"Epileptic whore hava yes, Major," smiled Mrs. Lee. "Velly clean, school teacher. Finest Kind."

Major Haskell perked his ears at the last expression, but before he could draw any conclusions Trapper started talking.

"Major," he said, "a guy in your business really should take a crack at this broad out of professional interest. It's an opportunity that's unlikely to come your way again. You could make a name for yourself writing papers about her."

The Major sat down, ordered a drink and excused the M.P.'s. "You may have a point, gentlemen. Can you fix me up? It should be quite an interesting case."

"The fastest ride in the Far East Command," Trapper assured him.

"And y'all may have my reservation," Duke told him. "I was on for three o'clock, but I can see that it'll mean more to you all."

"That's very kind of you, Captain," replied Major Haskell.

They had a few more drinks, ate an extended lunch, and at 3:00 P.M. Major Haskell went to keep his appointment.

"Good luck," said Trapper. "Don't break your stem."

"Y'all watch out when she sunfishes," warned Duke.

Within fifteen minutes the Major, looking somewhat pale

and drawn, reappeared and nervously ordered a double Scotch.

"That was quick," said Duke. "Major, y'all must be one of them short-time skivvy boys."

The Major did not reply.

"Come on, Major," urged Trapper, "how was it?"

"I don't think it's epilepsy. I think it's a purely hysterical convulsion," replied the Major.

"Yeah, but how was it?" insisted Duke.

"Tremendous," said the Major and departed.

For the next two days, business at Mrs. Lee's was big. The epileptic whore was in popular demand. The Swampmen hung around, observed with interest, interviewed many of the survivors, but did not avail themselves of her services.

On the second day, Hawkeye asked, "When are you guys gonna try her?"

"Maybe tomorrow," answered Trapper.

"What's the hurry?" asked Duke. "When y'all gonna try her yourself?"

"Never," said Hawkeye. "I'm a man of simple needs, which have already been adequately fulfilled for the time being."

On the third day Colonel Henry Blake, returning to his duties as C.O. of the 4077th MASH, stopped at the 325th Evac, called his outfit and requested transportation. He spoke to Colonel DeLong, who told him that the Swampmen were undergoing psychiatric evaluation at the 325th Evac.

Henry laughed with delight, but to himself. He sought out Major Haskell, who told him that McIntyre and Forrest were at Mrs. Lee's but that Pierce had dropped from sight.

"Don't worry, Major, they're all at Mrs. Lee's. I'll go over there. When my driver comes would you be kind enough to send him to pick us up?"

"I'm sorry, Colonel, but even if Pierce can be found, I couldn't possibly allow him to return to duty. I'm sure, when you see him, you'll agree with me."

151

"Pierce isn't any crazier now than he's ever been," Henry assured him. "Don't let him worry you, Major."

"I'll come with you if I may," said Haskell.

They found the Swampmen in Mrs. Lee's bar.

"Hiya, Henry. How they goin'?" asked Hawkeye. "I bet you got plenty in Tokyo, didn't you?"

"Shut up, Pierce. What's this all about?"

"I went ape," said Hawkeye, nodding to Major Haskell. "Ask him."

"I think you'd better come with me, Pierce," said Major Haskell.

Trapper joined in. "Henry doesn't believe you, Hawk. Say something in schizophrenic."

"My father was the keeper of the Eddystone light. He slept with a mermaid one fine night. Out of that union there came three—a porpoise and a porgy, and the other was me," replied Hawkeye.

"See what we mean?" said Duke.

Colonel Blake turned to Major Haskell. "I'll be responsible for him. Believe me, you've been had. Consider yourself lucky. I've been putting up with this kind of crap for months. You've only had a couple of hours of it."

Hawkeye summoned Mrs. Lee and whispered in her ear. Mrs. Lee asked to see the Colonel in private and led him upstairs to a certain room as Hawkeye ordered drinks for all and spoke to Major Haskell: "I hate to disappoint you, Dad, but I'm not quite as foolish as I led you to believe. I'm going back to the MASH with the rest of them as soon as Henry has enjoyed the Fastest Ride in the Far East Command. Have a drink with me, and let there be no moaning at the bar ere we leave Mrs. Lee."

"OK," said Haskell, "but I still don't think you're normal."

"I ain't. Normal people go crazy in this place."

While they were all on their second round of drinks, Colonel Blake returned.

152

"Well?" said Trapper John.

" 'Beware the Jabberwock, my son!' " said Colonel Blake, addressing Major Haskell, and then: " 'The jaws that bite, the claws that catch! Beware the Jubjub bird and shun the frumious Bandersnatch!' "

"Major," Hawkeye said to Haskell, "this looks like something right down your alley."

"Yeah, Major," the Duke said, "y'all been educated to handle this kinda thing, and we gotta get out of here."

12 With the end of summer, the baseball that the Swampmen had tossed and batted around occasionally to get some exercise and kill some time, took on air and a new shape. It became a football and an object of pursuit as, in their idle moments, they passed and kicked it back and forth and ran one another from one end of the ball field to the other to cries of: "How to go!"—"Nice grab!"—"Hawk, this time I'll fake to the Duke and you fake the block on the tackle and I'll hit you with it over the middle."—"Way to go!"—"Way to throw! Who ever heard of Sammy Baugh?"

"You know what we ought to do?" Hawkeye said, as they came puffing back into The Swamp one afternoon.

"Have a drink," the Duke said.

"No," Hawkeye said. "We oughta get us up a football team."

"And play who?" Duke said.

"The Chicago Bears," Trapper said. "It'd be a way to get home."

"No, thanks," Duke said. "I'd rather get killed over here."

154

"Listen, you guys," Hawkeye said. "I'm serious. We're all starting to get stirry again. We need something to do. There's that big guy named Vollmer over in Supply played center for Nebraska. Jeeter was a second string halfback at Oklahoma . . ."

"God help us," Trapper said.

"There's Pete Rizzo."

"He was a Three-I infielder," Duke said.

"But he played football in high school."

"But who do we play?" Duke said.

"Hot-Lips Houlihan's Green Bay Pachyderms," Trapper said.

"I want Knocko McCarthy on our side," the Duke said.

"Now, wait a minute," Hawkeye said. "I'm serious. They've got some kind of a league over here. The 325th Evac in Yong-Dong-Po claim they're champions because last year they beat two other teams. I know where we can get a real ringer, and if we can beat them we can clean up on some bets."

"You're nuts," Trapper said.

"Yeah," the Duke said, "and who's the ringer?"

"You ever hear of Oliver Wendell Jones?" asked Hawkeye.

"No," Trapper answered.

"Sounds like a nigra," said Duke.

"Never mind the racial prejudice. You ever hear of Spearchucker Jones?"

"Yeah," Trapper said.

"Maybe the best fullback in pro ball since Nagurski," Hawkeye said.

"Okay," Trapper said, "but what's he got to do with us?"

"You haven't read much about him lately, have you?" Hawkeye said.

"Probably just a flash," Duke said.

"Flash hell," Hawkeye said. "You want to know why you haven't heard about him?"

155

"Yeah," Duke said. "Tell us."

"No, don't tell us," Trapper said. "We'd like to spend all our spare time guessing."

"You haven't heard of Spearchucker Jones lately," Hawkeye said, "because his real name is Dr. Oliver Wendell Jones, and he's the neurosurgeon at the 72nd Evacuation Hospital in Taegu."

"Damn," Trapper said.

"Yeah," Duke said.

"But how come," Trapper, mixing the drinks now, wanted to know, "you're such an expert on all this?"

"Because," Hawkeye said, "when I was in Taegu before they dragged me kicking and screaming up here I roomed with Spearchucker. He went to some jerkwater colored college, but he did well enough to get into med school. He had played football in college, but no one had ever seen him. When he got out of med school he got married, and he wanted to take a residency. He needed some dough so he started playing semi-pro ball on weekends around New Jersey. Somebody scouted him and the Philadelphia Eagles signed him. He was great even though he couldn't work at it full time. He kept it a secret about being a doctor, but it would have leaked out fast if he hadn't been drafted just as he was getting a reputation."

"And you're the only one over here who knows this?" Trapper said.

"A few of the colored boys know who he is, but they won't talk because he's asked them not to."

"Good," Trapper said. "You really think we can get him?"

"Sure," Hawkeye said.

"Now, wait a minute," Duke said. "I know how you Yankees think. Y'all wanta get this nigra up here to live in The Swamp. Right?"

"Right," Hawkeye said.

"OK," Duke said. "If y'all can live with him, so can I. I'm

washed up at home anyway, after living with two Yankees."

"So how do we get him?" Trapper said.

"Easy," Hawkeye said. "We tell Henry we can't exist any longer without a neurosurgeon. If he doesn't go for that we tell him the truth. There's a little of the opportunist in Henry, too."

"Okay," Trapper agreed. "Let's make our run at him right now."

"But is this nigra in shape?" Duke wanted to know.

"This big bastard has to be a long way out of shape before anybody around here will stop him," Hawkeye assured him. "He's also a helluva guy."

Five minutes later Colonel Henry Blake, on his hands and knees on his tent floor, rummaging through his foot locker for some personal papers, was interrupted by the Swampmen who entered without knocking.

"Oops!" Trapper said, as Henry looked up. "Wrong address. This must be some kind of Shinto shrine."

"Looks like it," Hawkeye said. "Pardon us, oh Holy Man."

"Knock it off," Henry said, getting up. "What do you bastards want now?"

"A drink," Trapper said.

"You've got drinks where you live," Henry said, eyeing them. "What else do you want?"

"Here," Trapper said, handing Henry a Scotch, while Hawkeye and Duke helped themselves. "Relax."

"Henry," Hawkeye said, "you're not the only one caught up in this religious revival. We just had a revelation, too."

"What is this?" Henry started to say. "What . . . ?"

"Henry," Trapper said, "it just came to us. We gotta get us a neurosurgeon."

"Right," Duke said.

"You're out of your minds," Henry said.

"After all we've done for the Army," Trapper said, "is that too much to ask?"

157

"Please," Hawkeye said, genuflecting in front of Henry. "Please, oh Holy One, get us a neurosurgeon."

"We're serious," Trapper said.

"Right," Duke said.

"Okay," Henry said, still eyeing them. "What's the game?"

"Football."

"What?"

"Football."

"Football, hell," Henry said.

"We mean it," Hawkeye said, "and it's very simple. We want a football team, and we want to challenge the 325th Evac for the championship of Korea, and to do it we need a neurosurgeon. Wouldn't you like the 4077th MASH to be the football champions of Korea? Who knows? We might be invited to the Rose Bowl!"

"The hell with that," Trapper said. "Just think of the dough we can make, with a little judicious betting on ourselves."

"Explain," Henry said, perking up now. "And what the hell has a neurosurgeon got to do with it?"

"Ever hear of Spearchucker Jones?" Hawkeye said.

"Yeah. Colored boy. Plays pro football. So what?"

"He's not playing pro football right now, and we can get him."

"We can? How?"

"Tell General Hammond you gotta have a neurosurgeon, and you want Captain Oliver Wendell Jones of the 72nd Evac."

It took a moment for it to sink in.

"You mean it?" Henry said. "You really mean it?"

"You see?" Hawkeye said to the others. "I told you Henry believes in free enterprise, too."

"You're damn tootin'," Henry said. "You really think we can get him?"

"Sure," Hawkeye said. "Nobody else over here knows who he is, except a few of his friends who aren't talking."

"Good," Henry said, starting to pace the floor now. "Good thinking. Now you want to know something else?"

"What?"

"That Hammond," Henry said, pacing. "He flashes that star around and calls himself coach of that 325th Evac. Why, he's still back in the Pudge Heffelfinger era of football. He doesn't know the first damn thing about how the game is played today."

"Good," Trapper said.

"All he did was pull rank," Henry said.

"Then we can do it?" Hawkeye said.

"Yes," Henry said. "On one condition."

"What's that?"

"I want to be coach," Henry said.

"Anything you say, Coach," they assured him in unison.

"Hammond," Henry said. "Where'd he ever get the idea he's a coach?"

The next day Hawkeye composed a letter to Captain Oliver Wendell Jones, apprising him of the plan. He extolled the congenial working conditions at the Double Natural, described in glowing terms the friendly atmosphere of The Swamp, of which he invited Captain Jones to become the fourth member. Then he pointed out the benefits, financial as well as physical, that could accrue from playing a little football against the innocents of the 325th Evac. At the same time Colonel Henry Blake, chuckling to himself all the while, made the proper request to General Hamilton Hammond, and ten days later Captain Jones appeared, filling the doorway of The Swamp.

"My God!" Trapper said. "Darkness at noon. Look at the size of him!"

"And he drinks double bourbon and coke, Trapper," Hawkeye said, jumping up and shaking Captain Jones' hand. "Welcome, Spearchucker, welcome!"

"You sure I'm in the right place?" Captain Jones said, grinning.

159

"You sure are," Hawkeye said. "Shake hands with the Trapper. Shake hands with the Duke. Now shake hands with that double bourbon."

Captain Jones did. In fact, he shook hands with several double bourbons while the others made their usual display of affection for Trapper's martinis. Hawkeye and Captain Jones kicked around a few memories, and then Trapper John got into it.

"Tell me something," he said to Captain Jones. "Where'd you get that Spearchucker handle?"

"I used to throw the javelin," Jones told him. "Somebody started calling me that, and the sports writers thought it was good and it stuck."

"How come you and the Hawk here got to be such big buddies down in Taegu?"

"Well," said Jones, "I got assigned there and there weren't any other colored and they didn't have a room for me all by myself. Hawkeye went to the C.O. and said: 'Tell that big animal he can live with me if he wants to.'"

"That was nice," Trapper said, "but let's not give him the Legion of Merit."

"Nobody's handing out any medals," Spearchucker said, "but there are so goddamn many phonies around. The worst are the types who knock themselves out to show you that your color doesn't make any difference, and if it wasn't for your color they wouldn't pay any attention to you. They're part of the black man's burden, too."

"Understood," Trapper said.

"Anyway," Spearchucker said, "there are a lot of colored boys over here, and I know quite a few. Every now and then some of them would drop in to visit me. Now and then Hawkeye would stay around but most often he'd cut out. One day I said: 'Hawkeye, how come you don't care for some of my friends?'"

"So this guy," Spearchucker said, nodding toward Hawk-

160

eye, "says to me: 'Do you like all the white boys around here?' I said: 'No, Hawkeye, and thank you.' That's what I mean."

"The hell with this," Hawkeye said now. "Let's talk about something else."

"In a minute," the Duke said, and up to now he had been just monitoring the conversation. "I want to say something."

"What?" Spearchucker said, looking right at him.

"I'm from Georgia," Duke said.

"I know that," Spearchucker said.

"If you and I had a problem," Duke said, "we'd be the only ones who could understand it. These Yankees couldn't, but what I wanta say is that I don't have a problem, and if y'all do, tell me now."

Captain Jones sipped his drink and grinned and looked at the Duke.

"No problem with me, Little Duke," he said.

"Wait a minute," the Duke said, eyeing Captain Jones. "How come y'all call me Little Duke?"

"Well," Spearchucker said, "Hawkeye wrote me about you two guys and he said you're from Forrest City, Georgia. Right?"

"Right," Duke said, "but . . ."

"Your daddy a doctor?"

"Yeah."

"He used to own a little farm north of town?"

"Oh, no," Trapper John said. "Please."

"Wait a minute," Duke said. "He's right. Let the man talk."

"Who tenant-farmed that place?" asked Captain Jones.

"John Marshall Jones," Duke said.

"I should have been a lawyer," said Oliver Wendell Jones. "What happened to John Marshall Jones?"

"He got knifed by another nigra," Duke said.

"What happened to his family?"

"They went north."

"That's right," Captain Jones said. "They went north. You know where they got the money for the trip?"

"No."

"The doctor sold the farm, paid the family's debt and gave my mother a thousand dollars. They called him The Big Duke. Now how do you like that, Little Duke?"

Captain Forrest said nothing. He just sat there, looking at Captain Jones and shaking his head.

"You see why I got no problem?" Spearchucker said.

"Duke," Hawkeye said, "as Grant said to Lee at Appomattox: 'You give up?'"

"Yeah," the Duke said.

13 Colonel Henry Blake was busier than he had
been since The Deluge, and happier than he
had been since his arrival in Korea. The first thing he did
on the morning after his new neurosurgeon reported was
call General Hammond in Seoul and, still chuckling to himself, wonder if, by any chance, the football team of the 325th
Evacuation Hospital would care to meet an eleven repre-
senting the 4077th MASH.

General Hammond was delighted. The previous year his
team had administered such thorough hosings to the only two
pickup elevens in Korea foolish enough to challenge his
powerhouse that both of those aggregations had abandoned
the game. This had left him with a winning streak of two
straight, visions of some day joining the company of Pop
Warner, Amos Alonzo Stagg and Knute Rockne—and no one
to play. The date was set for Thanksgiving Day, five weeks
away, on the home field of the champions at Yong-Dong-Po.

The next thing Colonel Blake did was write Special
Services in Tokyo and arrange for the use of two dozen foot-

163

ball uniforms, helmets, shoes and pads, all to be airlifted as soon as possible. Then he dictated a notice, calling for candidates to report at two o'clock the next afternoon, and copies were posted in the messhall, the latrines, the showers and in the Painless Polish Poker and Dental Clinic. After that he showed up at The Swamp.

"Now," he said, after he had finished his report, "when do we start getting our dough down?"

"Why don't we wait a while, Coach," Trapper John suggested, "until we see what we've got for talent?"

"It doesn't matter what we've got," Henry responded. "That Hammond doesn't know anything about football."

"But if we seem too eager, Coach," Hawkeye said, "we may tip our hand."

"I guess you're right," Henry agreed.

The following afternoon, at the appointed hour, fifteen candidates appeared on the ball field. The equipment would not arrive for several days, so Henry, a whistle suspended from a cord around his neck, and as previously advised by his neurosurgeon, ran the rag-tag agglomeration twice around the perimeter of the field and then put them through some calisthenics. After that he just let them fool around, kicking and passing the three available footballs, while he and the Swampmen sized them up.

"Well," Henry said, at cocktail hour that afternoon in The Swamp, "what do you think?"

"Can we still get out of the game?" the Duke said.

"Yeah," Hawkeye said. "Whose idea was this anyway?"

"Yours, dammit," Trapper said.

"God, they looked awful," Hawkeye said.

"They'll look fine," Henry said, "once the uniforms get here."

"Never," the Duke said.

"Listen," Spearchucker said. "The coach is right. I don't mean particularly about the uniforms, but no team ever

164

looks good the first few days. I noticed a few boys out there who have played the game."

"Besides," Henry said, "what does that Hammond know about football? It's like having another man on our side."

"The first thing we've got to do," Spearchucker said, "is decide on an offense."

"That's right," Henry said. "That's the first thing we've got to do. What'll it be? The Notre Dame Box?"

Trapper had been a T quarterback at Dartmouth, and Duke had run out of the T as a fullback at Georgia. Androscoggin, where Hawkeye had played end, had still used the single wing, but Spearchucker had played in the T in college and, of course, with the pros. Hawkeye was outvoted, 3 to 1, with Henry abstaining but agreeing.

"Now we've got to think up some plays," Henry said. "Why don't you fellas handle that while I look after some of the other details?"

Spearchucker diagrammed six basic running plays and four stock pass plays, and that evening presented them to Henry, with explanations. Henry studied these, established a training table at one end of the mess hall and ordered his athletes to cut down on the consumption of liquor and cigarettes. The Swampmen settled for two drinks before dinner and none after, and reduced their inhalation of nicotine and tobacco tars by one half.

For the next two days, Henry, with surreptitious suggestions from Spearchucker, had the squad first walk through and then run through the plays. When the uniforms arrived they turned out, to the dismay of the Duke, who had worn the red for Georgia, to consist of cardinal jerseys, white helmets and white pants. As the personnel sorted through the equipment and found sizes that approximated their own, Henry fretted. He could hardly wait to see them suited up.

"Great! Great!" Henry exulted, as they lined up in front of him on the field. "You men look great!"

"We look like a lotta goddamn cherry parfaits," Trapper said.

"Great!" Henry went on. "Wait'll that Hammond sees you. He's in for the surprise of his life."

"It'll be the last surprise he'll ever have," the Duke said. "He'll die laughin'."

Things were not as desperate, however, as the Swampmen seemed to believe. To the practiced eye of their newest member, in fact, it was apparent that his colleagues possessed at least some of the skills needed to play the game. Trapper John, after he took the snap from center, hustled back and stood poised to throw, looked like a scarecrow, but he had a whip for an arm and began to regain his control. Hawkeye, when he went down for passes, exhibited good moves and good hands. The Duke had the short, powerful stride a fullback needs, ran hard, blocked well and, during the few semi-scrimmages, showed himself to be imbued with an abundance of competitive fire. Sergeant Pete Rizzo, the ex-Three I League infielder, was a natural athlete and a halfback. Of the others, the sergeant from Supply named Vollmer, who had played center for Nebraska, was the best. Ugly John made a guard of sorts and Captain Walter Koskiusko Waldowski, the Painless Pole, a survivor of high school and sandlot football in Hamtramck, was big enough, strong enough and angry enough to be a tackle. The rest of the line was filled out by enlisted men, with the exception of one of the end spots to which, over the objections of Trapper John, Dr. R. C. (Jeeter) Carroll was assigned.

The Spearchucker, of course, was kept under cover, except to jog around and catch a few passes. When anyone was watching he dropped them. No one guessed his identity, so scouts from the Evac Hospital could report to General Hammond only that the big colored boy was a clown, that whatever the Swampmen might have been once and were trying to be again, they had partaken of far too much whiskey and tobacco to go more than a quarter. Moreover, there were only four substitutes.

Hawkeye scouted the 325th. He went down one afternoon and tried to look like he was bound on various errands between the Quonsets that surrounded the athletic field, while he eyed the opposition.

"They got nothing," he reported on his return. "Three boys in the backfield looked like they played some college ball, but they probably aren't any better than Trapper, the Duke and me. They got a lousy passer, but their line is heavier than ours, and they got us in depth. I think that without the Spearchucker we could play them about even. With the Spearchucker they can't touch us."

"Good," Trapper said. "Then I suggest we do this: We hide the Spearchucker until the second half, and we hold back half our bets. We go into the half maybe ten points or two touchdowns behind, and then we bet the rest of our bundle at real odds."

"Great!" Henry said. "Everybody get his dough up!"

By the time everyone had kicked in—doctors, nurses, lab technicians, corpsmen, Supply and mess hall personnel— Henry had $6,000. The next morning—five days before the game—he called General Hammond, and when he came off the phone and reported to The Swamp it was apparent that he was disturbed.

"What happened?" Trapper asked. "Couldn't you get the dough down?"

"Yeah," Henry said. "I got $3,000 down."

"No odds?" Duke asked.

"Yeah," Henry said. "He gave me 7 to 5. He snapped it up."

"Oh-oh," Trapper John said. "I think I smell something."

"Me, too," Henry said. "That Hammond is tighter than a bull's ass in fly time. Whatever he's trying to pull, I don't like it."

"Tell you what we'd better do," Hawkeye said. "When I scouted those clowns they didn't look any better than we do but with them just as anxious to get their money down as we are, maybe I missed something. Spearchucker better go down tomorrow and nose around. He'll know a ringer if he sees one."

"Maybe I'd better go at that," Spearchucker said.

The next night Captain Jones returned from his scouting trip to Yong-Dong-Po. He didn't look any happier than Henry had the day before.

"What's the word?" asked Trapper John.

"They got two tackles from the Browns, and a halfback played with the Rams."

"That's not fair!" Henry said, jumping up. "Why, this game is supposed to be . . ."

"Wait a minute," Hawkeye said. "Are these guys any good?"

"Anybody ever ask you to play pro football, boy?" Spearchucker said.

"I get your point," Hawkeye said.

"My arm is sore," declared Trapper. "I don't think I can play."

"What do we do?" asked Henry.

"Y'all are the coach," Duke said. "How about it, Coach?"

"I guess we have to play," Henry said, his dreams of gold and glory gone.

"The bastards outconned us," Hawkeye said.

"Maybe not," Spearchucker said. "We'll think of something."

"Like what?" Duke said.

"Like getting that halfback out of there as soon as we can," Spearchucker said.

"You know him?" Duke said.

"No," Spearchucker said, "but I've seen him. He played only one year second-string with the Rams before the Army

168

got him. He's a colored boy who weighs only about 180, but he's a speed burner and one of those hot dogs."

"What does that mean?" Henry said.

"I mean," Spearchucker said, "that when he sees a little running room he likes to make a show—you know, stutter steps and cross-overs and all that jazz. He runs straight up and never learned to button up when he gets hit, so I think that, if you can get a good shot at him, you can get him out of there."

"Then let's kick off to them," the Duke said, "and get him right away."

"Good idea," Henry said.

"No," Spearchucker said. "He'll kill you in an open field. You've got to get him in a confined situation, where he hesitates and hangs up."

"Good idea," Henry said.

"Sure," Hawkeye said, "but how do we do that?"

"They'll run him off tackle a lot from strong right," Spearchucker said, "or send him wide. Hawkeye has to play him wide and turn him in, and when he makes his cut to the left he's gonna do that cross-over and Duke has to hit him high and Hawkeye low."

"Great idea!" Henry said. "That'll show that Hammond."

"Yeah," Duke said, "but can we do it?"

"It's the only way to do it," Spearchucker said. "If you don't get him the first time, he'll give you plenty of other chances."

"But when we unload him, if we can," Hawkeye said, "we'll have to break his leg to keep him from coming back in."

"Not necessarily," Trapper John said. "I got an idea."

"What is it?" Henry said.

"Tell you later," Trapper said, "if it works."

Trapper John excused himself, left The Swamp, walked over to Henry's tent and made a phone call. He talked for five minutes, and when he came back his teammates and their coach were dwelling on the problem presented by the two tackles from the Browns.

"We run nothing inside until I get into the game in the second half," Spearchucker was explaining. "These two big boys must be twenty or thirty pounds overweight. We run everything wide, except for maybe an occasional draw for Duke up the middle to take advantage of their rush on Trapper when he passes."

"God help me," Trapper said.

"And me, too," Duke said.

"In other words," Spearchucker said, "the idea is to run the legs off 'em that first half. I think that will be all the edge I will require, gentlemen."

"Right," Henry said. "Imagine that Hammond, trying to pull something like that."

On the day of Thanksgiving the kick-off was scheduled for 10:00 A.M., so shortly after the crack of dawn the 4077th MASH football team, the Red Raiders of the Imjin, all fifteen of them, plus their coach, their water boy and assorted rooters, took off in jeeps and truck. The Swampmen rode together in the same jeep and in silence. No bottle was passed and no cigarettes were smoked, and when they arrived in Yong-Dong-Po and headed for the Quonset assigned to the team as dressing quarters Trapper John excused himself and disappeared.

"Where the hell have you been?" Hawkeye asked him, when their quarterback finally returned just in time to suit up and loosen his arm.

"Yeah," the Duke said. "We thought y'all went over the hill."

"Had to see a man about a hot dog," Trapper said. "Good old Austin from Boston."

"Who?" Duke asked.

"About what?" Hawkeye said.

170

"Tell you about it if it works," Trapper said. "You two clods just take care of the halfback."

"All right, men," Henry was saying. "I want you to listen to me. Let's have some quiet in here. This game . . ."

He went into a Pat O'Brien-plays-Knute Rockne, stalking up and down and invoking their pride in themselves, their organization, the colors they wore and their bank accounts. When he finished, out of words and out of breath, his face was as red as their jerseys, and he turned them loose to meet the orange and black horde of Hammond.

"Look at the size of those two beasts," Trapper John said, spotting the two tackles from the Browns.

"We know," Duke said. "We were out here before. This is gonna take courage."

"I ain't got any," Trapper said.

"Me neither," Jeeter Carroll said.

"God help us," Trapper said.

Hawkeye, because it had been his idea to play the game in the first place, was sent out now, as captain, to face the two tackles for the coin toss. When he came back he reported that he had lost the toss and that they would have to kick off.

"Now keep it away from the speed-burner," Spearchucker instructed the Duke. "Kick it to anybody else but him."

"That's right," said Henry, regaining his breath. "Kick it to anybody else but him."

"I know," the Duke assured them. "Y'all think I'm crazy?"

"Let's go get 'em, men!" Henry said.

The Duke kicked it away from the halfback who had played a year of second-string with the Rams. He kicked it as far away from him as he could, but the enemy was of a different mind. The individual who caught the ball, by the simple maneuver of just running laterally and handing off, saw to it that the halfback who had played a year of second-string with the Rams got the ball. The next thing they knew, the Red Raiders of the Imjin saw an orange and black blur and

171

they were lining up to try to prevent the point after touch-down, an effort which also failed.

"Stop him!" Henry was screaming on the sidelines. "Stop that man!"

"Yeah," the Duke was saying as they distributed them-selves to receive the kick-off. "Y'all give me a rifle and I might stop him, if they blindfold him and tie him to a stake."

When the kick came, it came to the Duke on the ten and he ran it straight ahead to the thirty before they brought him down. On the first play from scrimmage Trapper sent Hawkeye, playing at left half until Spearchucker could get into the game, around right end. Hawkeye made two yards, and Pete Rizzo, at right half, picked up two more around the other flank.

"Third and six," Hawkeye said, as they came back to huddle. "I'll run a down and out."

"I'll run a down and in," Jeeter Carroll said, "but throw it to Hawkeye."

"My arm is sore," Trapper said.

"Y'all gotta throw," Duke said.

"God help us," Trapper said.

By the time he had taken the snap and hustled back, Trap-per John knew that his blocking pocket had collapsed. He knew it because the two tackles from the Browns were de-scending upon him, and he ran. He ran to the right and turned and ran to the left.

"Good!" Spearchucker was calling from the sidelines. "Run the legs off those two big hogs!"

"Throw it!" Henry was shouting. "Throw it!"

Trapper threw it. Hawkeye caught it. When he caught it he lugged it to the enemy forty-nine. That was about as far as that drive went, and with fourth and five on the forty-four, Duke went back to punt.

"Don't try for distance," Hawkeye told him. "Kick it up there so we can get down and surround that sonofabitch."

"Yeah," Duke said, "if I can."

He kicked it high and, as it came down, the halfback who had played a year of second-string with the Rams, waiting for it on his twenty, saw red jerseys closing in. He called for a fair catch.

"A hot dog," Spearchucker said, on the sidelines. "A real hot dog."

"A hot dog," Hawkeye said to Duke as they lined up. "Spearchucker had him right."

"Yeah," Duke said. "Let's try to take him, like the Chucker said."

When the play evolved, it was also as Spearchucker had called it. The halfback who had played a year of second-string with the Rams went in motion from his left half position, took a pitch out, turned up through the line off tackle and tried to go wide. When he saw Hawkeye, untouched by blockers, closing in from the outside, he made his cut. He made that beautiful cross-over, the right leg thrust across in front of the left, and just at the instant when he looked like he was posing for the picture for the cover of the game program, poised as he was on the ball of his left foot, the other leg in the air and one arm out, he was hit. From one side he was hit at the knees by 200 pounds of hurtling former Androscoggin College end, and from the other he was hit high by 195 pounds of former Georgia fullback.

"Time!" one of the former Brown tackles was calling. "Time!"

It took quite some time. In about five minutes they got the halfback who had played a year of second-string with the Rams on his feet, and they assisted him to the sidelines and sat him down on the bench.

"How many fingers am I holding up?" General Hammond, on his knees in front of his offensive star and extending the digits of one hand, was asking.

"Fifteen," his star replied.

"Take him in," the General said, sadly. "Try to get him ready for the second half."

173

So they took him across the field and into the 325th Evac. As the Swampmen watched him go, Trapper John was the first to speak.

"That," Trapper John said, "takes care of that. Scratch one hot dog."

"Y'all think he's hurt that bad?" the Duke asked.

"Hell, no," Trapper said, "but we won't see him again."

"I suspect something," Hawkeye said. "Explain."

"An old Dartmouth roomie of mine," Trapper explained, "is attached to this cruddy outfit. I called him the other night, after Spearchucker outlined the plot, and told him to put in for Officer of the Day today."

"I'm beginning to get it," Hawkeye said.

"This morning," Trapper went on, "I paid him a visit and cut him in for a piece of our bet. Right now Austin from Boston is going to place that hot dog under what is politely called heavy sedation, where he will dwell for the rest of the game and probably the rest of the day."

"Trapper," Hawkeye said, "you are a genius."

"Y'all know something?" the Duke said. "I think we can beat these Yankees now."

"Time!" the referee was screaming, between blasts on his whistle. "Do you people want to play football or talk all day?"

"If we have a choice," Hawkeye said, as they started to line up, "we prefer to talk."

"But you ain't got a choice," one of the tackles from the Browns said, "and you'll get yours now."

"What do y'all mean?" the Duke said. "It was clean."

"Yeah," Hawkeye said, "and you'll have to catch us first."

On that drive the enemy was stopped on the seven, and had to settle for the field goal that made it 10–0. For their part, the Red Raiders devoted most of their offensive efforts to pulling the corks of the two tackles, running them from one side of the field to the other. Midway in the second

174

quarter they managed a score after Ugly John had fallen on a fumble on the enemy nineteen. Two plays later Hawkeye caught a wobbling pass lofted by a still fleeing Trapper John and fell into the end zone. Just before the end of the half the home forces rammed the ball over once more, so the score was 17–7 when both sides retired for rest and resuscitation.

"Very good, gentlemen," Spearchucker, who had been pacing the sideline helmeted and wrapped in a khaki blanket, told them as they filed in. "Very good, indeed."

"Yeah," Trapper John said, slumping to the floor, "but I gotta have a . . ."

". . . beer, sir?" said Radar O'Reilly, who had been serving during the time-outs as water boy.

"Right," Trapper said, taking the brew. "Thank you."

"Tell you what," Hawkeye said. "They got us now by ten, so we ought to be able to get two to one. Coach?"

"Yes, sir?" Henry said. "I mean, yes?"

"You better get over there quick," Hawkeye said, "and grab that Hammond and try to get the rest of that bundle down at two to one."

"Yes, sir," Henry said. "I mean, yes. What's the matter with me, anyway?"

"Nothin', Coach," Duke said. "Y'all are doing a real fine job."

Henry was back in less than five minutes. He reported that he had failed to get as far as the other team's dressing room. Halfway across the field he had been met by General Hammond who, having just checked on the health of his offensive star, had found him still under sedation. As Henry described him, the General was extremely irate.

"He was so mad," Henry said, "that he wanted to know if we'd like to get any more money down."

"Did you all tell him yes?" Duke wanted to know.

"He was so mad," Henry said, "that he said he'd give us three to one."

"And you took it?" Trapper said.

"I got four to one," a gleeful Henry said.

"Great, Coach!" they were shouting now. "How to go, Coach!"

"But," Henry said, the elation suddenly draining from his face, as he thought of something, "we still have to win."

"Relax, coach," Spearchucker assured him. "If these poor white trash will just give me the ball and then direct their attentions to the two gentlemen from Cleveland, Ohio, I promise you that I shall bring our crusade to a victorious conclusion."

Henry gave them then a re-take of his opening address. He paced the floor in front of them, waving his arms, exhorting, praising, pleading until, once more, his face and neck were of the same hue as their jerseys and once more, and for the last time, he sent them out to do or die.

As the Red Raiders of the Imjin distributed themselves to receive the kick-off, Captain Oliver Wendell Jones took a position on the goal line. The ball was not kicked to him, but the recipient, Captain Augustus Bedford Forrest, made certain that he got it. Without significant interference, Captain Jones proceeded to the opposite end zone. Captain Forrest then kicked the extra point, bringing the score up to 17–14, and while the teams dragged themselves back upfield, the two tackles from the Browns were seen loping over to their sideline. There they were observed in earnest conversation with General Hamilton Hartington Hammond who, as the two lumbered back onto the field, was seen shaking his fist in the direction of Lieutenant Colonel Henry Braymore Blake.

"Those two tackles, sir," Radar O'Reilly informed his colonel, "told General Hammond that they recognize Captain Jones, sir."

"Roll it up!" Henry, ignoring both his corporal and his general, was screaming. "Roll it up!"

"Keep it down," advised Hawkeye. "We may want to do this again."

"We may not have to worry about that," Spearchucker, still breathing heavily, informed them. "I guess I'm not in the shape I thought I was. This may still be a battle."

It was. It was primarily a battle between the two tackles and Spearchucker, with certain innocent parties, such as Ugly John and the Painless Pole and Vollmer, the sergeant from Supply and center from Nebraska, in the middle. When the Red Raiders got the ball again they went ahead for the moment, as Spearchucker scored once more on a forty yard burst, but then the enemy surged back to grind out another and, with three minutes to play the score was Hammond 24, Blake 21, first-and-ten for the home forces on the visitors' thirty-five-yard line.

"We gotta stop 'em here," Spearchucker said.

"We need a time-out," Trapper John said, "and some information."

"Time-out!" Hawkeye called to the referee.

"Radar," Trapper John said, when Radar O'Reilly came in with the water bucket and the towels, "do you think you can monitor that kaffee-clatch over there?"

He nodded toward the other team, gathered around their quarterback.

"I think I can, sir," Radar said. "I can try, sir."

"Well, goddammit, try."

"Yes, sir," Radar said, fixing his attention on the other huddle.

"What are they saying?"

"Well, sir," Radar said, "the quarterback is saying that they will run the old Statue of Liberty, sir. He's saying that their left end will come across and take the ball off his hand and try to get around their right end."

"Good," Spearchucker said. "What else are they saying?"

"Well, sir," Radar said, "now the quarterback is saying that, if that doesn't work, they'll go into the double wing."

"Good," the Duke said.

"Ssh!" Hawkeye said. "What are they gonna do out of the double wing?"

"Well, sir," Radar said, "they're having an argument now. Everybody is talking so it's confusing."

"Keep listening."

"Yes, sir. Now one of the tackles is telling them all to shut up. Now the quarterback is saying that, out of the double wing, the left halfback will come across and take the hand-off and start to the right. Then he'll hand off to the right halfback coming to the left."

"Radar," Hawkeye said, "you're absolutely the greatest since Marconi."

"Greater," Trapper John said.

"Thank you, sir," Radar said. "That's very kind of you, sir."

"Time!" the referee was calling. "Time!"

It was as Radar O'Reilly had heard it. On the first play the enemy quarterback went back, as if to pass. As he did, the left end started to his right, and the Red Raiders, all eleven of them, started to their left. The left end took the ball off the quarterback's hand, brought it down, made his cut and met a welcoming committee of ten men in red, only Ugly John, temporarily buried under 265 pounds of tackle, failing to make it on time.

"Double wing!" Spearchucker informed his associates as the enemy lined up for the next play. "Double wing!"

"Hut! Hut!" the enemy quarterback was calling. "Hut!"

This time the left halfback took the hand-off and started to his right. The eleven Red Raiders started to *their* right and, as the right halfback took the ball from the left halfback, ran to his left and tried to turn in he, too, was con-

178

fronted by ten men wearing the wrong colors. This time it was the Painless Pole who, tripping over his own feet, kept the Red Raiders from attaining perfect attendance.

The first man to hit the halfback was Spearchucker Jones. He hit him so hard that he doubled him over and drove him back five yards, and as the wind came out of the halfback so did the ball. It took some time to find the ball, because it was at the bottom of a pile of six men, all wearing red jerseys.

"Time!" Spearchucker called, and he walked over and talked with the referee.

"What's the matter?" Trapper John asked him, when he came back. "Let's take it to them."

"Too far to go, and we're all bushed," Spearchucker said. "I just told the referee that we're gonna try something different. We're gonna make the center eligible by . . ."

"Who?" Vollmer, the sergeant from Supply and center from Nebraska said. "Me?"

"That's right," Spearchucker said. "Now everybody listen, and listen good. We line up unbalanced, with everybody to the right of center, except Hawkeye at left end. Just before the signal for the snap of the ball, Duke, you move up into the line to the right of the center and Hawkeye, you drop back a yard. That keeps the required seven men in the line, and makes the center eligible to receive a pass."

"Me?" Vollmer said. "I can't catch a pass."

"You don't have to," Spearchucker said. "Trapper takes the snap and hands the ball right back to you between your legs. You hide it in your belly, and stay there like you're blockin'. Trapper, you start back like you got the ball, make a fake to me and keep going. One or both of those tackles will hit you . . ."

"Oh, dear," Trapper said.

"Meanwhile," Spearchucker said to Vollmer, "when your man goes by you, you straighten up, hidin' the ball with your arms, and you walk—don't run—toward that other goal line."

179

"I don't know," Vollmer said.

"You got to," Hawkeye said. "Just think of all that dough."

"I suppose," Vollmer said.

"Everybody else keep busy," Spearchucker said. "Keep the other people occupied, but don't hold, and Vollmer, you remember you walk, don't run."

"I'll try," Vollmer said.

"Oh, dear," Trapper John said.

"Time!" the referee was calling again. "Time!"

When they lined up, all of the linemen to the right of the center except Hawkeye, they had some trouble finding their positions and the enemy had some trouble adjusting. As Trapper John walked up and took his position behind the center and then Duke jumped up into the line and Hawkeye dropped back, the enemy was even more confused.

"Hut!" Trapper John called. "Hut!"

He took the ball from the center, handed it right back to him, turned and started back. He faked to Spearchucker, heading into the line, and then, his back to the fray, he who had once so successfully posed as The Saviour now posed as The Quarterback With the Ball. So successfully did he pose, in fact, that both tackles from the Browns and two other linemen in orange and black fell for the ruse, and on top of Trapper John.

Up at the line, meanwhile, the sergeant from Supply and center from Nebraska had started his lonely journey. Bent over, his arms crossed to further hide the ball, and looking like he had caught a helmet or a shoulder pad in the pit of the stomach and was now living with the discomfort, he had walked right between the two enemy halfbacks whose attention was focused on the trapping of Trapper John. Once past this checkpoint, about ten yards from where he had started and now out in the open, the sergeant, however, began to feel as conspicuous as a man who had forgotten his pants, so

180

he decided to embellish the act. He veered toward his own sideline, as if he were leaving the game.

"What's going on?" Henry was screaming as his center approached him. "What's going on out there? What are you doing?"

"I got the ball," the center informed him, opening his arms enough for Henry to see the pigskin cradled there.

"Then run!" Henry screamed. "Run!"

So the sergeant from Supply and center from Nebraska began to run. Back upfield, the two tackles from the Browns had picked up Trapper John. That is, each had picked up a leg, and now they were shaking him out like a scatter rug, still trying to find the ball, while their colleagues stood around waiting for it to appear, so they could pounce on it. Downfield, meanwhile, the safety man stood, shifting his weight from one foot to the other, scratching an armpit, peering upfield and waiting for something to evolve. He had noticed the center start toward the sidelines, apparently in pain, but he had ignored that. Now, however, as he saw the center break into a run, the light bulb lit, and he took off after him. They met, but they met on the two-yard line, and the sergeant from Supply and center from Nebraska carried the safety man, as well as the ball, into the end zone with him.

"What happened?" General Hammond, coach, was hollering on one sideline. "Illegal! Illegal!"

"It was legal," the referee informed him. "They made that center eligible."

"Crook!" General Hammond was hollering at Lieutenant Colonel Blake on the other sideline, shaking his fist at him. "Crook!"

"Run it up!" Henry was hollering. "Run it up!"

"Now we just gotta stop 'em," Spearchucker said, after Duke had kicked the point that made it MASH 28, Evac 24.

"Not me," Trapper John said, weaving for the sideline.

181

And stop them they did. The key defensive play was made, in fact, by Dr. R. C. (Jeeter) Carroll. Dr. Carroll, all five feet nine inches and 150 pounds of him, had spent the afternoon on the offense just running passroutes, waving his arms over his head and screaming at the top of his lungs. He had run button-hooks, turn-ins, turn-outs, zig-ins, zig-outs, posts and fly patterns. Trapper John had ignored him and, after the first few minutes, so had the enemy. Now, with less than a minute to play, with the enemy on the Red Raiders' forty, fourth and ten, Spearchucker had called for a prevent defense and sent for the agile Dr. Carroll to replace Trapper John.

"Let's pick on that idiot," Radar O'Reilly heard one of the enemy ends tell the enemy quarterback as Jeeter ran onto the field. "He's opposite me, so let's run that crossing pattern and I'll lose him."

They tried. They crossed their ends about fifteen yards deep but the end couldn't lose Jeeter. Jeeter stuck right with him but, with his back to play, he couldn't see the ball coming. It came with all the velocity the quarterback could still put on it, and it struck Jeeter on the back of the helmet. When it struck Jeeter it drove him to his knees, but it also rebounded into the arms of the Painless Pole who fell to the ground still clutching it.

"Great!" Henry was shouting from the sideline. "Great defensive play."

"That's using the old head, Jeeter," Hawkeye told Dr. Carroll, as he helped him to his feet.

"What?" Jeeter said.

"That's using the old noggin," Hawkeye said.

"What?" Jeeter said.

Then Spearchucker loafed the ball into the line twice, the referee fired off his Army .45 and they trooped off the field, into the waiting arms of Henry, who escorted them into their dressing quarters where they called for the beer and slumped to the floor.

"Great!" Henry, ecstatic, was saying, going around and shaking each man's hand. "It was a great team effort. You're heroes all!"

"Then give us our goddamn Purple Hearts," said Ugly John, who had spent most of the afternoon under one or the other of the two tackles from the Browns.

When General Hammond appeared, he was all grace. In the best R.A. stiff-upper-lip tradition he congratulated them, and then he took Henry aside.

"Men," Henry said, after the general had left, "he wants a rematch. Whadda you say?"

"I thought he was bein' awful nice," Spearchucker said.

"We might be able to do it to them again," Henry said, still glowing.

"Never again," Hawkeye said. "They're on to us now."

"Gentlemen," the Duke, slumped next to Hawkeye, said, "I got an announcement to make. Y'all have just seen me play my last game."

"You can retire my number, too," Trapper John said.

"Mine, too," Hawkeye said.

"Anyway, men," Henry said, "I told you so."

"What?" Hawkeye said.

"That Hammond," Henry said. "He doesn't know anything about football."

14

For the next two days, Henry spent his spare time distributing the profits of the betting coup to the financial backers of the Red Raiders. The way the money had been bet—half of it before the game at two to one and the rest at halftime at four to one—meant that the ultimate payoff was three to one, so when Henry stopped off at The Swamp on the second afternoon and handed each of the occupants his original $500 and then $1,500 more, the recipients were more affluent than they had been in a long while.

"And no place to spend it," the Duke said.

"Send it home," the colonel advised.

"No," Hawkeye said. "I got a better idea."

"What?" Henry said.

"You keep all the money, and send *us* home."

"No chance," Henry said.

"But why, coach?" Duke wanted to know. "With the time the Hawk and me put in before they sent us to y'all, we been over here longer than anybody but you."

"That's right," Hawkeye said, "and it ain't fair."

"Excuse me," Trapper John said, getting up, "but I've heard this before and I don't want to hear it again."

"I'll go with you," Spearchucker said. "I can't stand the sight of suffering, either."

"Soreheads!" the Duke called after them. "Just because we get out before y'all!"

"Seriously, Henry," Hawkeye said, "the Duke and I are scheduled to get shed of this Army in March. That's only a little over three months away. Now, ever since we've been stuck out here at the tag end of nowhere we've watched a procession of our contemporaries come and go. Singles and doubles hitters, strike-out artists, long down the fairway or off into the woods, it didn't matter what they were, because they all got rotated back to stateside duty four–five months before they were to get sprung."

"That's right," Henry said.

"But why?" the Duke said.

"I know why," Hawkeye said. "It's because the Army always gets even."

"What do you mean?" Henry said.

"I mean," Hawkeye said, "that the Duke and I are two of the three biggest screwups over here, or four if you count Roger the Dodger . . ."

"I don't count him," Henry said. "I don't even think of him, and if that sonofabitch comes around here again I'm gonna have him shot on sight."

"Anyway," Hawkeye said, "you gotta admit it. We screwed up, so now the Army, defender of democracy and symbol of justice, is gonna take it out on us."

"No," Henry said. "You're wrong. You won't believe it, but it's not a punishment."

"Then what is it?" the Duke said. "It feels like a punishment."

"It's ironic," Henry said, "but it's because you two, like

185

Trapper John, came here with more than average training and experience. You've done a good job when the chips were down, and now we can't afford to waste you. If you went home now you'd be of no use to anyone but your wives. Therefore, we've got to keep you here until your enlistments expire."

"Ain't that the damndest thing?" the Duke said.

"In short," Hawkeye said, "we screwed up in the wrong area. If we had dubbed it along in the working time and never given it the goddamn college try, we'd be back at some stateside hospital, living with our wives and behaving like officers and gentlemen? Is that right?"

"Yeah," agreed Henry with a broad grin.

"I couldn't stand a stateside Army hospital," the Duke said. "Too many jerks."

The next morning the two appeared in front of Colonel Blake's tent. When the colonel came out in answer to their calls, they announced that the Spearchucker had arranged for them both to be given $25,000 bonuses by the Philadelphia Eagles and they were leaving immediately for the City of Brotherly Love. They then departed by jeep, and were neither seen nor heard from for three days. Colonel Blake, of course, was aware that the other two occupants of The Swamp knew where they were and could have them back in two hours if a hint of heavy work arose.

Four days after they returned, the two, whose previous escapade had been ignored by Henry, appeared once again in front of their colonel's tent. Once again he went out to meet them.

"So where do you wise bastards think you're going this time?" he inquired.

"Paris," replied Hawkeye.

"Yeah," said the Duke.

"That's very interesting," said Henry. "What for?"

"We gotta get the Duke fixed," explained Hawkeye. "It's

186

an emergency. He's been nice to me and Trapper and Spearchucker for three days in a row, and we think he's turnin'."

"Well," said Colonel Blake, "that certainly is an emergency, and we can't have that sort of thing around here, but why don't you just take him down to Seoul? It's so much closer."

"Why, Colonel," replied Hawkeye, "you can't be serious. Just two days ago you gave the enlisted men a lecture on how they should not get it in Seoul because there is so much neisserian infection. What applies to enlisted men must certainly apply to officers, and we do not wish to set a bad example. We hear that there is not too much of it in Paris, so that's where we are going."

With that they jumped into their jeep and disappeared for what turned out to be another three days. This time their colonel realized that, for the good of the organization if for no other reason, he would have to curtail the extracurricular excursions of his two transients. At the same time he realized that, as the two sweated out the termination of their enlistments and grew more itchy by the day, he needed some means of keeping them busier and thus happier in their home away from home. He might have prayed for an increase in battle casualties, but he was too fine a human being for that, so he prayed for any other answer, and the next morning it appeared in two parts, named Captains Emerson Pinkham and Leverett Russell.

Captains Pinkham and Russell were replacements for two of Henry's surgeons who, having been nursed along to the point of being able to accept major responsibility, had unaccountably but not unexpectedly been whisked away. Henry greeted them, oriented them and then invited them to meet him and various members of his staff late that afternoon for cocktails at the so-called Officers' Club.

It was a pleasant, but in some ways disturbing, social occasion and confrontation. Trapper John, Spearchucker, Ugly

John and the others who were not on duty found Captains Pinkham and Russell highly presentable. They were intelligent, polite, seemed to possess normal senses of humor and on the subject of surgery talked impressively. This last should not have surprised nor disturbed the veterans, for the surgical world changes rapidly and almost all surgical residents talk well, but the veterans had been so far removed from the mainstream of their profession for so long that, as the recruits expounded on new approaches and new techniques, at least several of the listeners wondered if, when they did get home, they would have to start all over again.

"Well," Henry said, as he, Trapper John and Spearchucker headed toward the mess hall at the party's end, "they seem all right. Good men."

"I think so," Spearchucker said, "for Ivy League types."

"I guess so," Trapper John said, "but we'll see what the Hawk and the Duke think, if they ever get back."

"Oh, they'll be back," Henry said, "and that gives me an idea."

Two days later, when Hawkeye and the Duke returned, Henry read them the Old Familiar. While the strains of that were still sounding in their ears, he launched into his project for the preservation of what remained of the sanity of Hawkeye and the Duke and the perpetuation of the efficiency of his organization.

"Now, while you two clowns were gone," he told them, "we picked up two new men. Their names are Emerson Pinkham and Leverett Russell."

"Sound like Ivy League types," Duke said.

"That's right," Henry said. "They are, but they're good men. They're intelligent, they've had excellent training and they're abreast of certain new concepts of surgery that you and I have never even heard about."

"Good," Hawkeye said. "Then let them do all the work."

"No, goddammit," Henry said, the red rising to his hairline again. "Not for one minute. That's been the trouble with this organization. When we've been busy there hasn't been time to teach the new men the kind of hurry-up, short-cut or call-it-what-you-will surgery that you have to do in a place like this. When we've had time you people have goofed off, which is my fault, and as a result anybody who learned anything here just picked it up by accident. Well, that's gonna stop, and it's gonna stop right now. These new men are going to be taught everything they can be taught, and you two are gonna teach them!"

"Yes, sir," Duke said.

"OK," Hawkeye said. "I guess you're right."

At lunch that day, Henry introduced Hawkeye and Duke to Captains Emerson Pinkham and Leverett Russell, and the two veterans invited the two recruits to join them, Trapper John and Spearchucker at The Swamp for cocktails at four o'clock. At four o'clock the two appeared and were served libations. As before, they shaped up well in all the requisite areas. Since their arrival they had observed a number of operations and had performed two themselves, and this, of course, quite naturally invited a comparison between the methods being employed at the MASH and the techniques taught in the high-level stateside training hospitals.

"I think I can speak for Lev as well as myself," Captain Pinkham said at one point, "when I say that we are not, for a moment, regretting our presence here. There's a job to be done, and some men are giving their lives so, at the very least, we can give our time and our talents, such as they may be. At the same time, any surgeon, aware of everything that's going on in his field back home, has to regret it when he's sent to a place like this where about all he ever gets to do is meatball surgery. No offense, of course."

Hawkeye looked at Duke, Duke looked at Hawkeye, Trapper John and Spearchucker looked at their colleagues. The term was one that was used often in The Swamp, but now it had just been used by someone else, and a recruit.

"No offense," Hawkeye said. "Have another drink."

As it happened, the Double Natural was moderately busy at this time, and Henry had paired Captains Pinkham and Russell with Captains Pierce and Forrest on the night shift. On this very first night, in fact, there was even a six o'clock chopper, so after they had bolted down a quick meal, the two veterans escorted the two recruits over to view the passengers.

The chopper had brought two 4077th MASH Specials: both had belly and extremity wounds, and one had a minor chest wound. Hawkeye and Duke stood back while Captains Pinkham and Russell made their examinations, then informed the recruits that they would be ready and willing to assist when the patients had been prepared and moved into the OR. After that the two Swampmen retired to the lab where, a few minutes later, Captain Bridget McCarthy found them avidly engaged in questioning Radar O'Reilly who had recently been in communication with Jupiter.

"All right, you two!" Captain McCarthy ordered. "Get out of here!"

"What's your maladjustment tonight, Knocko?" asked Hawkeye.

"Listen," she said. "Your two Cub Scouts want to operate on those patients right away, and they're not ready to be operated on."

"Now just a minute, ma'am," Duke said. "Just where did y'all . . ."

"Attend medical school?" Knocko asked. "Right here."

"Yes, ma'am," Duke said. "We'll go help."

In the preoperative ward the two graduates of the ivory tower surgical training programs were showing their inexperience. The two cases that confronted them were well within the ability of the Double Natural, or any other MASH,

190

to handle. Both patients were in moderate shock, but had no continuing blood loss. Both required preoperative resuscitation by a process well known even to the corpsmen and Korean helpers.

Captain Pinkham had the boy with the minor but significant chest wound. When Hawkeye and Duke wandered in, he was fussing around the patient, rapping on the chest and listening to it with a stethoscope. He was behaving, in other words, like a doctor and not a meatball surgeon, so Hawkeye took a look at the X-ray, assessed the situation and spoke.

"Doctor," he said, "this guy obviously has holes in his bowel and his femur is broken. It's not a bad fracture, but he's probably dropped a pint here. There's at least a pint in his belly and maybe a pint in his chest. Agreed?"

"Agreed," Captain Pinkham said.

From there Hawkeye went on to explain that the patient also had a pneumothorax, meaning that there was air in his pleural, or chest, cavity because his lung was leaking air and had collapsed. In addition, he suggested, the shock from the blood loss was probably augmented by contamination of the peritoneum, or abdominal, cavity by bowel contents.

"So what he needs," he said, "before you lug him in there and hit him with the Pentothal and curare and put a tube in his trachea, is expansion of his lung, two or three pints of blood and an antibiotic to minimize the peritoneal infection."

"I see," Captain Pinkham said, beginning to see a little light, "but we'll still have to open his chest as well as his belly."

"No, we won't," said Hawkeye. "The chest wound doesn't amount to a damn. Stick a Foley catheter between his second and third ribs and hook it to underwater drainage, and his lung will re-expand. If he were going to do any interesting bleeding from his lung, he'd probably have done it by now. We can tap it after we get the air out and his general condition improves. Right now we just want to get this kid out of shock and into the OR in shape to have his belly cut and his thigh debrided."

Two corpsmen brought what at the Double Natural passed for an adequate closed thoracotomy kit. It contained the bare essentials for insertion of a tube in a chest, and after Hawkeye had watched Captain Pinkham fiddle around with it for awhile, he spoke again.

"Look," he said. "All that's great, but there will be times when you won't have the time to do it right. Lemme show you how to do it wrong."

Hawkeye donned a pair of gloves, accepted a syringe of Novocain from a corpsman, infiltrated the skin and the space between the ribs and shoved the needle into the pleural cavity. Pulling back on the plunger he got air, knew he was in the right place, noted the angle of the needle, withdrew it, took a scalpel, incised the skin for one-half inch and plunged the scalpel into the pleural cavity. Bubbles of air appeared at the incision. Then he grasped the tip of a Foley catheter with a Kelly clamp and shoved the tube through the hole. A nurse attached the other end to the drainage bottle on the floor, a corpsman blew up the balloon on the catheter and now bubbles began to rise to the surface of the water in the bottle. Hawkeye dropped to his knees on the sand floor and, as he began to suck on the rubber tube attached to the shorter of the two tubes in the bottle, the upward flow of bubbles increased as the lung was, indeed, expanding.

"Crude, ain't it?" said Hawkeye.

"Yes," said Captain Pinkham.

"How long did it take?"

"Not long," admitted Captain Pinkham, who couldn't help noticing that the patient's breathing had already improved.

Duke, meanwhile, watched Captain Russell apply his surgical resident's approach to the other soldier who, waiting for blood, was still in shock. Captain Russell, afraid that he'd miss something, was examining the patient centimeter by centimeter, fore and aft, while the corpsmen waited impatiently to start the transfusion.

"Excuse me," Duke said after a while, "but all you're doin' now is holdin' up progress. Why don't y'all let these folks get to work?"

"But don't you think . . ." Captain Russell started to say.

"What I think," Duke said to the corpsmen, "is that we better start the blood."

Having taken the recruits that far, the two veterans headed for the game in the Painless Polish Poker and Dental Clinic to pass the two hours until the patients would be ready for surgery. When they figured that the patients had been sufficiently transfused and adequately resuscitated, they headed back to the OR, scrubbed and joined their junior partners.

Duke and Captain Russell had a boy whose small bowel was somewhat perforated, requiring removal of two different areas and closure of several individual holes. This sort of work is done ritualistically in most surgical training programs, because it is basic to belly surgery and should never be learned incorrectly, and as a result, the surgical residents in their third and fourth years of training, particularly in good teaching hospitals, may still be at the ritualistic stage. Captain Russell surely was.

Duke, having determined that all they had to do was fix the small bowel and that time, up to a point, was not going to be a factor, decided to sweat it out. For two hours he stood there amusing himself by mildly insulting Knocko McCarthy, who wouldn't hurt him while he was scrubbed, and assisting in wonder as Captain Russell performed a small bowel resection as performed by the residents in a large university hospital.

"Do y'all mind if I do this one?" he asked, as Captain Russell finally advanced on the second area needing repair. "I

193

lost twenty bucks in that poker game, and I'll never get even at this rate."

He didn't wait for an answer. In twenty minutes he removed the damaged segment of bowel and sewed the two ends together.

"Y'all probably noticed," he explained to Captain Russell as they were closing, "that when clamping and cutting the mesentery, I wasn't quite as dainty as y'all were. Y'all will recall that I didn't do the anastomosis with three layers of interrupted silk, like y'all did. I used an inner layer of continuous catgut and interrupted silk in the serosa. Where y'all put twelve sutures on the anterior side of yours, I put four. Y'all observed that the lumen in my anastomosis is as big as yours, I've got mucosa to mucosa, submucosa more or less to submucosa, muscularis pretty much to muscularis and serosa to serosa, and there ain't any place where it's gonna leak. It took y'all two hours, and it took me twenty minutes. Your way is fine, but y'all can't get away with it around here. Y'all will kill people with it, because a lot of these kids who can stand two hours of surgery can't stand six hours of it."

"But . . ." Captain Russell started to say.

"That's right," Duke said, "and if I'm really in a hurry I'll ride with just the continuous catgut through all the layers."

So it went, for several weeks. The recruits, being polite, listened and, being intelligent, learned. They had both, however, been born and bred, as well as formally educated, to be fastidious, so the shucking of old habits did not come easily. Captain Pinkham, in particular, still tended to get bogged down in detail. He would become completely absorbed in repairing damage to a hand and ignore or sublimate the obvious fact that the patient could die of his abdominal wounds. Once, in fact, on a busy night while Hawkeye was occupied elsewhere, he spent six hours on a case that should not have taken more than two hours and

194

managed to miss a hole in the upper part of the stomach. The patient almost died, early, from too much surgery and, later, from the missed hole. Hawkeye took that one back to the table and, two days later, with the patient well on the way to recovery, he was able to make this the case in point.

"Now I'll offer you some thoughts," he told the much relieved Captain Pinkham. "This is certainly meatball surgery we do around here, but I think you can see now that meatball surgery is a specialty in itself. We are not concerned with the ultimate reconstruction of the patient. We are concerned only with getting the kid out of here alive enough for someone else to reconstruct him. Up to a point we are concerned with fingers, hands, arms and legs, but sometimes we deliberately sacrifice a leg in order to save a life, if the other wounds are more important. In fact, now and then we may lose a leg because, if we spent an extra hour trying to save it, another guy in the preop ward could die from being operated on too late.

"That's hard to accept at first," he said, "but tell me something, doctor. Do you play golf?"

"I do," Captain Pinkham said, "but I haven't been getting much in lately."

"Then let me put it this way," Hawkeye said. "Our general attitude around here is that we want to play par surgery on this course. Par is a live patient. We're not sweet swingers, and if we've gotta kick it in with our knees to get a par that's how we do it."

"I can't argue against that," Captain Pinkham said.

"Good," Hawkeye said. "Come on up to The Swamp for a drink."

Colonel Blake, of course, was enormously pleased. He had not only hit upon a project that was at least partially intriguing Captains Forrest and Pierce during their final months, but also Captains Pinkham and Russell were obvi-

195

ously benefitting. He had established a kind of teaching hospital. Then Captain Pinkham came to see Colonel Blake and Colonel Blake came to see Captain Pierce.

"Have a drink, Henry," Hawkeye said.

"Yeah," the Duke said. "Join us."

"No, thanks," Henry said. "How's it going?"

"Good," the Duke said. "Can we go home now?"

"No," Henry said. "What I want to know is how Pinkham's been doing lately."

"Good," Hawkeye said, "although the last couple of days I've had the feeling that I'm starting to bore him."

"He's got a problem," Henry said.

"We all have," Hawkeye said.

"Not like his," Henry said.

"What's wrong with him?" the Duke said.

"His wife," Henry said.

"Too bad," Hawkeye said, "but he married the broad. You didn't, so why is he bothering you?"

"Yeah," the Duke said.

"Ever since he landed here," Henry said, "he's been getting letters from his wife saying she can't live with his parents and their kid is sick, she thinks, but the doctor doesn't, and why doesn't he come home and take her off the hook? The damn fool woman seems to think the guy can break it off over here any time he wants to."

The two Swampmen were silent. Henry looked from one to the other.

"Come on, you guys," he said. "You always got ideas. What the hell am I going to do? I didn't think I was sent over here to run a kindergarten."

"If I was y'all," said Duke, "I wouldn't do a goddamn thing."

"Sure," Henry said. "That's the obvious answer, but I have a hospital to run and you know how hard replacements are

196

to get, and I have to make the ones we get as useful as I can. This guy was just starting to shape up, but this week he got four letters, all saying the same thing but each one worse than the one before. She'll drive him nuts."

"I don't know," Hawkeye said.

"Me neither," Duke said.

"Thanks a lot," Henry said, as he departed.

The next day Captain Pinkham received another and more desperate letter from his wife. This time he didn't tell anyone about it, but at 2:00 A.M. it was obvious to Hawkeye, who was watching him closely, that Captain Pinkham was trying to concentrate but that he was failing. Between cases he gave the Duke the word and they took Captain Pinkham to The Swamp, gave him a beer and asked: "What's the trouble? Anything we can do?"

Captain Pinkham showed them the letter. After reading it, they took him to his tent, gave him a sleeping pill and said: "Sleep and don't worry about the work."

The next day Captain Pinkham awakened still impaled on the horns of the kind of trouble only hardnoses can survive, and Captain Pinkham was no hardnose. Two days later, fortunately for all, salvation came. It came to Colonel Blake, via the Red Cross and the Army, in the form of orders to send Captain Pinkham home on emergency leave. His wife had folded and been placed in a private fool farm.

The two Swampmen found that they missed Captain Pinkham, who had proved himself willing to try, so they were particularly nice to Captain Russell, who missed his buddy even more. Between themselves the two made noises about how they would handle that kind of grief if it ever came their way, but they both had the same doubts. They thanked their good fortune for wives who didn't bug them from 9,000 miles away, and they sat down and wrote identical letters:

Darling,

I love you. I need you, I hope you love me and need me. If so, you can have me in two weeks by following these simple instructions:

(1) Go crazy.

(2) Notify the Red Cross.

Love,

15

The days passed, among them Christmas and New Year's. On Christmas, Dago Red said four Masses at nearby troop concentrations, another at the Double Natural where he also conducted a non-denominational service. Then he pulled all the strings behind the scenes at the party in the mess hall where a red-suited and white-bearded Vollmer, the sergeant from Supply and center from Nebraska, a pillow strapped to the stomach where the ball had once been cradled, handed out clothing, cigarettes and fruit to a gaggle of Korean house boys while their benefactors among the personnel of the 4077th applauded.

For dinner on both holidays, Mother Divine put down excellent repasts. Mother, still president of the Brooklyn and Manhattan Marked-Down Monument and Landmark Company, and still doing business with Caucasians from south of the Mason-Dixon Line, was in a beneficent mood. For a while during the autumn, business had slackened off, but the onset of the holiday season had brought on a gift-buying stampede, and Mother had even managed to unload two items in which little interest had previously been shown.

The first of these was the Soldiers' and Sailors' Monument at 89th Street and Riverside Drive. It was purchased by a Private First Class from Hodge, Alabama, who mailed the postcard picturing it to his fiancée, with the following message printed on the reverse side:

Huney:
    I just bot this for you. They will delivur it in a cuple weeks. Have them put it in yur side yard and wen we get marreed I'll get Puley to help me muve it to our own place.
    Merry Xmas. Your frend and husbend to be.

His buddy, and near-hometown-neighbor from Dutton, bought Fifth Avenue (Looking North From Forty-Second Street) as a surprise for his father. On the back of the card, circa 1934, he wrote:

Pa:
    Merry Christmus. I bout this strete for you. You can see that all of the cars that use it are olden, so I figger you can move the garege up there and will get all the busines you can handel. I'll help wen I get home. Merry Christmus agan.

The holidays over, time dragged for Hawkeye and Duke. The 4077th was reasonably busy, so they had enough to do. When Henry was afraid they didn't, and still on his teaching hospital kick, he had them shepherding associates with less experience over the rocky pastures of meatball surgery, until one night, early in February, he entered The Swamp, kicked the snow off his boots, helped himself to a large shot of Scotch, made himself comfortable on one of the sacks and announced to Captains Forrest and Pierce: "I've got orders for you two eightballs to ship out of here a week from today."

200

Duke and Hawkeye jumped, laughed, hugged Henry, hugged each other. Spearchucker, with two months left to go, congratulated them warmly. In the far corner of the tent, Trapper John McIntyre with almost six months of servitude still ahead of him, lay on his sack and looked at the roof.

The last week was interminable. Preparation for leaving involved very little so, considering the importance of the event, The Swamp was pretty quiet. Finally, Duke and Hawkeye shaped up for their last night shift, and the demands it made upon them brought them back to earth.

Arterial injuries were not unusual, but this night they caught two. Trying to save the right leg of a G.I. from Topeka, Kansas, and the left leg of a Tommy from Birmingham, England, Duke and Hawkeye did two vein grafts to bridge the arterial gaps blown out by gook artillery. When the shift was over, they started for The Swamp, tired, excited, and troubled. They had just done two operations on two legs belonging to young men, to each of whom a leg was important, and they were walking away knowing that, in all probability, they would never learn the fate of the legs.

At The Swamp, their two colleagues were waiting for them, bottle open. By 11:00 A.M. they had gone over for the third time plans, which each secretly suspected would never materialize, for meeting in the States as soon as possible after Spearchucker and Trapper John gained their releases.

"Look," Trapper John said finally, "aren't you guys going to say goodbye to Henry?"

"Naturally," Duke said. "We take kindly to the man."

"Well, why don't you do it now?"

"Yes, father," Hawkeye said.

At 11:15 A.M. Duke and Hawkeye, still in their soiled fatigues but wearing scrubbed and serious looks, arrived at the office of Colonel Henry Blake. Hawkeye approached Henry's sergeant, threw his shoulders back and stated, "Captain Pierce and Captain Forrest request permission to speak to Colonel Blake."

The sergeant, who had known them for eight months as Duke and Hawkeye, was shaken.

"What kind of bullshit is this?" he wanted to know. "Don't screw up now, for Chrissake."

"Don't worry," Hawk assured him. "Announce us."

The sergeant knocked on Henry's door and announced: "Captain Pierce and Captain Forrest request permission to speak to the Colonel."

Colonel Blake blanched. His knees shook.

"What are they up to?"

"Don't know, Sir."

"Well, let's find out. Send them in."

Duke and Hawkeye entered, saluted and stood at attention.

"Stop it, you two! Cut it out!" roared Colonel Blake. "You're making me nervous. What the hell have you got in mind now?"

"Tell him, Duke," Hawkeye, still at attention, said.

"You all tell him. I can't."

"Well, Henry," explained Hawkeye, "we haven't come to apologize for anything exactly . . ."

"Good," Henry said.

". . . but we wanted you to know that we know what you've had to put up with from us and that we appreciate it. We think you're quite a guy."

Duke stepped forward and offered a much-relieved but silent Henry his hand. Hawkeye also shook hands, and then they saluted, executed a perfect about-face and, solemn-faced and in step, departed.

Back at The Swamp, most of the outfit had showed up for a farewell drink. Ugly John, who would drive them to Seoul in the jeep, was there. So were Dago Red and the Painless Pole, Jeeter Carroll, Pete Rizzo, Vollmer, the sergeant from

Supply and center from Nebraska, and the other survivors of the Thanksgiving Day Massacre, officers and enlisted men all milling around in a heterogeneous mass. Captain Leverett Russell thanked them for their patience during the past months. Radar O'Reilly presented them with his own version of their horoscopes. Mother Divine, who had just leased out the rowboat concession for the Central Park Lake, sent over a box lunch for them to take along, and Colonel Blake appeared just long enough to hand over two bottles of Scotch to be put in the jeep. Everyone wished them luck, pumped their hands, and gave them home addresses.

"Let's get the hell out of here," Hawkeye whispered to the Duke, finally. "I'm beginning to feel like Shaking Sammy."

"Me, too," the Duke said.

Hawkeye looked toward Trapper John's corner. Trapper had a bottle and a glass. He sat on the edge of his sack, alternately taking large gulps of the liquid and letting his head drop almost into his lap. Hawkeye went over, took the bottle and glass and put them on the washstand.

"All right, you bastards!" he announced to the others. "Out! We leave in two minutes."

The others pushed their way through the door, and the bottle was reclaimed from the washstand. The Duke poured four drinks, which were downed in silence. The Duke shook hands with Spearchucker and Trapper and left without a word. Hawkeye Pierce shook hands with Spearchucker, and then stuck out his hand for Trapper John.

"Hang in there," he said.

"Get the hell out of here," Trapper John said.

Outside, Ugly John waited at the wheel of the jeep, the others gathered around it. Hawkeye and Duke climbed into the back seat and, as Ugly John gave it the gun and they affected Nazi salutes, they made their turbulent departure from the cheering multitude.

"Don't look back," Hawkeye said.

"I ain't," the Duke said.

For five minutes the two did not look at each other, nor did they speak. Their first act to break the silence was to blow their noses.

"Well," said the Hawk finally, "when you live in this sort of situation long enough, you either get to love a few people or to hate them, and we've been pretty lucky. I don't know. I do know that nothing like this will ever happen to us again. Never again, except in our families, will we ever be as close with anyone as we were in that goddamned tent for the past year, and with Ugly here and Dago and a few others. I'm glad it happened, and I'm some jeezely glad it's over."

"Yeah," agreed the Duke, "and y'all know what I'm thinkin'? We came in a jeep, half in the bag, and now we're leavin' in a jeep, half in the bag."

In Seoul, the jeep carrying Captains Duke Forrest and Hawkeye Pierce and driven by Captain Ugly John Black found its way to an Air Force Officers' Club.

"I can't believe it. I just can't believe we're actually goin' home," Duke kept saying, as they stood at the bar.

"You lucky bastards," groaned Ugly. "I don't know if I can hold out one more month."

"You'll make it, Ug," Hawkeye said.

"Yeah," the Duke said. "It's good y'all came this far with us to see how it's done."

They had a supper of shrimp cocktail and filet mignon. Hawkeye, in fact, had two shrimp cocktails, two filet mignons, and pondered ordering a third round.

"You got worms?" Ugly wanted to know. "You hit those steaks like they're going to bite back if you don't swallow them fast."

"You mean these appetizers? Jesus, boy, you oughta see the meal my old man and the valedictorian will have for me when I get home!"

Dinner finally over, they returned to the bar. As they sipped their brandies, the conversation, which had been lagging, came to a halt.

"Let's finish these up and haul for where we spend the night," Hawkeye said finally. "I'm tired."

"Well," said Ugly, "when am I ever going to see you guys again?"

"Ugly," answered Hawk, "that's a painful subject. I hope it's soon, but I don't know. If you come to Maine, you'll see me. If we attend the same medical meetings we'll meet. From here it sounds great to say we'll all get together soon, but all I know is this: You can call me or the Duke fifty days or fifty years from now and we'll be glad to see you."

"Right," the Duke said.

"Yeah," Ugly said. "I know what you mean."

Ugly drove them to the Transient Officers' Quarters at the 325th Evacuation Hospital, from opposite ends of which, more than fifteen months before, the two had emerged to meet for the first time. They watched the jeep disappear into the darkness and head north and back to the Double Natural.

They opened the door of the Transient Officers' Quarters, walked in, stomped the snow off their feet and dumped their barracks bags on the floor. Looking around they saw a dismal but familiar military scene. A large room was almost filled with triple-decker bunks. The floor was littered with old copies of *The Stars and Stripes* and empty beer cans. There were two weak electric lights hanging from the ceiling, two bare wooden tables and a few flimsy chairs. In a corner, five young officers were seated around one of the tables talking earnestly, seriously, worriedly. Their clean fatigues and their general appearance indicated that they were coming, not going.

Duke selected one of the three-decker bunks. He examined it carefully, prodding it and poking it.

"Hawkeye," he said, "I think y'all better pour us some prophylactic snake bite medicine. This place is plumb full of snakes."

"I never argue about snakes with a man from Georgia," said Hawkeye, extricating a bottle and paper cups from his bag. "I will pour the necessary doses."

They sat at the wooden table, sipped the Scotch, smoked, and said little but looked happy. They had long hair, could have used shaves, and their clothes were dirty. Between them they owned one-half pair of Captain's bars, which Hawkeye wore on the back of his fatigue cap.

From the corner, the eager new officers watched them with interest. Finally one of them rose and approached.

"May I ask you gentlemen a question?" he inquired.

"Sure, General," said Hawkeye, who had turned his fatigue cap around so that the Captain's bars showed.

"I'm not a general, Captain. I'm a lieutenant. May I ask why you wear your cap that way?"

"What way?"

"Backwards."

Hawkeye took his cap off and inspected it.

"It looks OK to me," he said. "Course, I ain't no West Pointer, and frankly I don't give a big rat's ass whether it's on backwards or forwards. What's more, when I wear it this way, a lotta people think I'm Yogi Berra."

"Yogi Berra?" the lieutenant said.

"Hey, Duke," Hawkeye ordered. "Gimme my mask."

The lieutenant scuffed his feet and asked, "How long have you gentlemen been in Korea?"

"Eighteen months," Duke informed him. "Seems like just yesterday we came."

The lieutenant left and rejoined his group. "They're nuts," he told them.

"Jesus," said one of them, "I hope we don't look like that after eighteen months."

"Hawkeye," Duke said, "y'all hear what that boy said?"

206

"Yeah."

"Do y'all attach any significance to it?"

"Not much. We've done our jobs. I'm not ashamed of anything. I don't care what anyone thinks."

"Me neither," Duke said, "but y'all don't suppose we've really flipped, do you? Sometimes I'm not sure."

"Duke, wait'll you see your wife and those two girls. You'll be tame, docile and normal as hell. I wouldn't know you two months from now. Relax."

"Yeah," Duke said, pouring another drink, and then raising his voice, "but do y'all know something? This is the first day in eighteen months I ain't killed nobody."

"Like hell! You didn't get one on Christmas."

"That's right. I forgot, but y'all know it kind of gets in your blood. Guess I'll clean my .45 just in case any Chinks infiltrate this here barracks."

The Duke took out his .45, started to clean it and to look significantly at the new officers in the other corner. He poured another drink. "Hawkeye," he announced loudly, "those guys are Chinks in disguise, or at least I think they are. Guess I'll shoot 'em, just to be safe."

Hawkeye got up, his hat on backwards, and approached the new officers.

"Maybe you guys better cut out for a while," he suggested. "I only think I'm Yogi Berra, but my buddy has a more serious problem. After four drinks he knows he's the United States Marines."

Duke started to sing as he loaded his .45:

From the Halls of Montezuma
To the Shores of Okefenokee.

The new officers went through the door rapidly and into the snow. They found the 325th Evacuation Hospital's Officers' Club. If they hadn't been green, they'd have found it sooner. Excitedly, to an enthralled audience that included

Brig. General Hamilton Hartington Hammond, the five described their experiences in the barracks.

"Leave those two alone!" General Hammond thundered, when someone suggested that the Military Police be summoned. "For Chrissake, just leave them alone! Just hope that train leaves in the morning with them on it. Assign these men other quarters!"

Ere long, Duke and Hawkeye grew lonesome.

"You scared our friends," said Hawk. "They left."

"Yeah," Duke said, "but that ain't important. I just don't believe that y'all are Yogi Berra. I ain't the United States Marines, either, because I'm Grover Cleveland Alexander. Let's get that buddy of Trapper John's who's stationed here to find us a catcher's mitt. Then y'all can warm me up at the Officers' Club."

"Grover," Hawkeye said, "I think you got a fast ball like Harriet Beecher Stowe."

"What's Trapper's friend's name?" Duke said, ignoring him.

"I don't know," Hawkeye said. "I think he called him Austin From Boston."

"Good," the Duke said. "There can't be two people named that."

They finished their drinks and went out into the night. For forty-five minutes they tramped through the snow, traversing the various roadways while, at the top of their voices, they called for Trapper John's friend.

"Austin From Boston!" they called. "Oh, Austin From Boston! Where are you, Austin From Boston, Trapper John's friend?"

Their cries, of course, penetrated the Officers' Club where, at the bar, the five new men clustered now around General Hammond. They were afraid to request an armed escort to accompany them to their new quarters, and they were even

208

more afraid of going out in the snow and dying alone so far from home.

"Goddammit, you men!" General Hammond said finally, tiring of playing mother hen as they pressed closer around him with each plaintive cry. "Why don't you go to your quarters and get some rest?"

"It must be terrible up there, Sir," one of the new men said.

"Up where?" General Hammond said, starting to swing his elbows now.

"Up at the front, Sir."

"Oh, Goddammit," the General said, giving up. "Do your mothers know you're over here?"

"Yes, Sir," they all replied.

Unable to find Trapper John's friend, who may well have heard their calls and wisely decided against responding, Hawkeye and Duke returned to the barracks where, as soon as they hit their bunks, they fell into sound slumber. Three hours later, Hawkeye was awakened by the Duke, who was fully dressed and fully packed. This had required very little effort, as he had neither undressed nor unpacked.

"Wake up, y'all. We're goin' home. That train leaves at seven."

"What time is it now?"

"Four."

"Jesus, are you out of your mind? I wanna sleep."

"Y'all can't sleep. I think we both got snakebit during the night. Have some medicine."

He handed Hawkeye a shot of Scotch and a lighted cigarette. While Hawkeye immunized himself, Duke filled a flask.

"The mess hall starts servin' at four-thirty," he announced. "We gotta eat hearty."

As soon as the mess hall opened, Duke and Hawkeye entered with barracks bags and proceeded to eat heartily. Over a cup of coffee, Hawkeye reached into a seldom used pocket for a fresh pack of cigarettes. With the cigarettes came a small piece of paper. On it was written, in the unmistakable hand of Trapper John McIntyre, the unmistakable poetry of Bret Harte:

> Which I wish to remark,
> And my language is plain,
> That for ways that are dark
> And for tricks that are vain,
> The heathen Chinee is peculiar,
> Which the same I would rise to explain.

And then: "It's a small place, and now I love it less. If the heathen Chinee should get lucky, just remember your old Dad, and know that he wouldn't have missed it for the world."

Hawkeye handed the note to Duke who read it and took out his flask. They drank reverently and headed for the nearby train.

The train ride to Pusan was a full twelve-hour journey. The two Swampmen slept for the first six hours; then Hawkeye read while Duke gazed out the window. At one point a sergeant of the Military Police, patrolling the aisle, requested politely that Hawkeye remove his captain's bars from the back of his fatigue cap and pin them on the front and Hawkeye, to his own surprise, politely acceded.

"Well, now," Duke said, after the sergeant had gone on. "For a much-decorated, fierce, front-line fighting type like y'all, that was pretty peaceful. Y'all goin' chicken?"

"No," Hawkeye said, "but I've been thinking."

"It give you a headache?"

"I've been thinking that you and I really have been living a life that few of the people we're gonna meet from here on in know anything about. Most of the combat and near front-line people like us fly out from Seoul, so we're gonna look like freaks to the clerk-typists and rear echelon honchos who have been living about as they would in a stateside Army camp. We'd better act at least half civilized. In fact, it wouldn't hurt if, the next chance we get, we even put on clean uniforms."

"I'll think about it," agreed Duke.

In Pusan they were directed to the Transient Officers' Quarters and assigned to one of the Quonset huts. The hut was divided into three compartments, and they were in one of the end divisions. Each area was heated by an oil stove, and each cot had a mattress on it.

"Which reminds me of something else," Hawkeye said, as they examined their quarters.

"What's that?" Duke asked.

"I am reminded," Hawkeye said, "that back in The Swamp you were one of the most faithful observers of the night rules. Religiously you would leave your sack, walk three steps to the door and take the seven prescribed paces before initiating micturition. This is such a conditioned habit that I thought I'd mention it. It might not be appropriate tonight."

"I'll bear that in mind, too. Anythin' else, Aunty?"

Although the rest of the Quonset filled rapidly, there were, among the other guests, few other medical officers and none from MASH units. There were few people who had been up forward, so Duke and Hawkeye were satisfied to keep to themselves. After a reasonable number of drinks and at a reasonable hour, they decided to hit their sacks, but after fifteen months on hard cots a mattress atop a spring may seem uncomfortable. Duke, having tried his, dragged his mattress to the floor, where he went to sleep until approximately 3:00 A.M., when Hawkeye was awakened by a loud voice complaining in the next compartment.

211

"Hey, buddy," someone was protesting, "you can't do that in here!"

"I'm doin' it, ain't I?" Captain Pierce heard Captain Forrest reply, and shortly Captain Forrest returned to flop down on his mattress again and begin to snore once more, as the occupants of the next compartment continued to grumble and complain.

In the morning it was clear that their fellow officers considered Duke inapproachable. With misgivings they sought out Hawkeye and registered their complaints. Since neither Duke nor Hawkeye wore medical insignia, Hawkeye saw no reason to correct the impression that he and Duke were fierce, battle-hardened combat veterans. He was pleasant but firm.

"I'll do my best," he assured the committee, "but even I dassn't rile that man none. If I can get him home without him killin' anybody, or earnin' the Purple Heart for myself, I'll be lucky. He's got so he can't hardly tell a Chink from anyone else."

As Hawkeye finished his explanation, Duke joined the group and at the same moment a passing truck backfired. Hawkeye and the Duke hit the floor, simultaneously drawing their .45's and looking around for the enemy. Then, realizing their mistake, they arose, feigning embarrassment.

That night Hawkeye slept without interruption. When he awoke it was to the babble of another delegation of their neighbors, standing in the doorway and viewing with obvious distaste the Duke, still sleeping on his mattress on the floor.

"What's the matter?" Hawkeye, sitting up and rubbing the sleep from his eyes, asked him. "He didn't do it on the floor again, did he?"

"No, he did it on the stove."

"Why didn't you stop him?"

"We were afraid he'd do it on us."

That afternoon they embarked aboard a ferry for Sasebo. As the ferry left the dock, they leaned over the side, smoking and observing a crowd of Koreans and a Korean band cheering and serenading their departure. Hawkeye threw his cigarette into the swirling, dirty waters below.

"And now," he said, "as we leave the Beautiful Land of Korea, the grateful natives line the shores and chant: 'Mother ————, Mother ————.'"

"Y'all just about said it all," agreed the Duke.

As the ferry approached the Japanese shore, Sasebo materialized from the mist as a pretty town. There were mountains, evergreens and a rocky shoreline that, not that he needed any prodding, reminded Hawkeye of the coast of Maine. There were shops and Officers' Clubs and several thousand troops awaiting transportation home. The Swampmen abandoned fatigue uniforms, donned Ike jackets, adorned them with proper insignia and became recognizable as medical officers.

This was a mistake. Before any group of returnees was allowed to board a troopship, short-arm inspection was mandatory, and properly so. Returning medical officers were drafted for this duty, and when the Swampmen heard about this, they were shaken.

"Not me," said Hawkeye. "Let the pill rollers who been doing it all along do it. After eighteen months of being one of their knife artists, I ain't going to be demoted."

"Me neither," declared Duke.

A sergeant with a pad descended upon them. "You men medical officers?" he asked.

"Yes."

"May I have your names, please?"

"What for?"

"I'm making up the roster for short-arm inspection tomorrow."

"Oh, certainly, Sergeant," Hawkeye said. "My name is

Captain George Limburger, and this is Captain Walter Camembert."

The sergeant started to write, and Hawkeye politely assisted him with the spelling.

"What time tomorrow?" Duke asked.

"You'll be notified."

Time passed slowly in the big, bare barracks. No one seemed to know when they'd ship out. After being placed on the short-arm roster, the Swampmen decided to go shopping. Popular items in the local shops were flimsy, transparent negligees known as skin suits. No red-blooded American boy wanted to return to his homeland without several skin suits for his loved one, or ones, and the local shopkeepers were hard put to meet the demand.

"I gotta get me some skin suits," said Hawkeye.

"Me too."

At the nearest shop they looked over the selection. The Duke insisted on having one with fur, preferably mink, around the bottom. After much haggling and consultation between employees and owners, the shop agreed to supply such a garment if given twenty-four hours. Their command of English didn't match their curiosity, and they couldn't completely grasp the Duke's simple explanation that he did not wish his wife's neck to get cold.

The next morning the sergeant who came in search of Captains Limburger and Camembert was a different sergeant. He went through the barracks shouting: "Limburger! Camembert?" Several officers inquired about the price. Some asked for crackers. The sergeant became annoyed. Finally he arrived in the area occupied by Duke and Hawkeye, who had just returned from shaving and had yet to don shirts or insignia.

"What do you want with those two guys?" Hawkeye asked him.

"They're supposed to hold short-arm inspection."

214

"You can't be serious!"

"Why not?"

"Don't y'all know," said Duke, "that those guys are the two biggest fairies in the Far East Command? That'll be the longest short-arm inspection y'all ever saw."

The sergeant perceived the logic of their argument. He consulted his list. "You know anybody named Forrest or Pierce?" he inquired.

"Yeah," Duke told him. "They shipped out yesterday."

"Well, thanks a lot," said the sergeant.

Two days later the word came. They were to board a Marine transport for Seattle. They packed. They had a bottle of V.O. left, and booze was not allowed on troopships.

"What difference does it make?" asked Hawkeye. "How we going to get enough booze on board to last us to Seattle, anyway?"

"I got an idea," the Duke said. "Let's drink this jug and have our next drink in Seattle. If we can go that long without it, we'll know we're not dangerous alcoholics."

"The first sign of a stewbum," said Hawkeye, "but it's OK with me."

They boarded ship carrying pretty full loads. Having been informed that short-arm inspection was also carried out at regular intervals on shipboard, they checked in under their own names, but then assumed new identities. The Caduceus of the Medical Corps was removed from the Eisenhower jackets. The simple cross of the Chaplain's Corps replaced it.

They shared a cabin with four other returning officers who were not particularly pleased to find two chaplains among them. The conversation was slightly stilted until, that evening, Duke and Hawkeye broke the ice.

"Do you gentlemen happen to have any Aureomycin?" asked Hawkeye. "The Reverend here seems to be developing a slight cold. In fact, gentlemen, the Reverend, I fear, has fallen from grace with a large splash."

215

"What do you mean?" asked one of their cabin-mates.

"The Reverend, God forbid, has come down with the clap."

Incipient laughter was cut short by a stern look from Hawkeye. "Be charitable, gentlemen. Help us. My colleague is a good man. It is just that he has been unusually bedevilled, and I must do something to remedy the tragic results of his excessive libido before he returns to Kokomo, where he is betrothed to the Bishop's daughter. Bishops, as a group, are opposed to gonorrhea, and this one has particularly firm views on the subject."

Meanwhile Duke, looking very pleased, began to leaf through a girlie magazine, a corner of which he had noticed protruding from a barracks bag.

"Stop looking at those pictures, Reverend," commanded Hawkeye.

One of the group, a big, tough, rough-looking first lieutenant, with the crossed rifles of the infantry on his collar and the look of the front line about him, was observing them quizzically. After a little more of the act, he began to grin.

"They ain't no chaplains," he exclaimed in a broad southern accent. "They're Duke and Hawkeye from the 4077th MASH. They saved my brother's life two months ago. What the hell's wrong with you guys?"

"We are traveling incognito," Duke told him. "We will do anything to avoid officiating at short-arm inspection, and we figure if we are chaplains there will be no one demanding that we view three thousand weapons."

"Yeah," quibbled one of them, "but they must have your names. It's a big boat, but in two or three weeks they're bound to track you down."

"Any of you guys want to be Forrest and Pierce of the U. S. Army Medical Corps between here and Seattle?" asked Hawk. "Tell you what we'll do. We'll pay you."

"How much?"

"Cent for each one you inspect."

"Pretty low wages," one of them, a red-haired artillery captain from Oregon, said.

"But it's an important contribution to public health," Hawkeye told him.

"I'll do it for two cents a weapon," the infantry man who had recognized them said, "not a penny less."

"You are hired," Hawkeye informed them, handing them their medical insignia. "You are now members of the Army Medical Corps."

"How do we go about it?" inquired the new physicians.

"It is very simple," Hawkeye explained. "You get a chair. You sit on it backwards with your arms clasped behind its back and your chin resting on the top. You gotta have a big cigar in your mouth. You just sit there and look. Most of the guys will know what to do. If they don't you growl, 'Skin it and wring it, soldier.' Sound mean when you say it. If you think there is a suspicion of venereal disease, you make a gesture with your thumb like Bill Klem calling a guy out at the plate. Then somebody hauls the guy off somewhere. I never found out what happens to them. Every now and then, just so they know you're alert, you grunt, 'Don't wave it so close to my cigar, Mac!' If you follow these simple rules, you can't go wrong."

Just to be safe, Duke and Hawkeye kept the chaplains' insignia on their collars. Other doctors didn't interest them, and medical insignia invited medical conversation. However, the chaplains' roles soon became as burdensome. One Lutheran parson from central Pennsylvania was particularly interested in talking shop. He asked Duke what his reaction had been to his Korean experience. Duke cured him quickly. "Loved it," he answered. "Didn't do nawthin' but hoot, holler, drink rum and chase that native poon!"

On the fourth day out they became captains in the Medi-

217

cal Corps again. Their two new friends had established themselves as short-arm inspectors, and they themselves had tired of being asked for spiritual guidance by soldiers who had flunked inspection.

"Now I know what happens to the guys who get thumbed out of the short-arm line," said Hawk. "They get a shot of penicillin and a ticket to see the chaplain."

The time passed slowly, but it did pass. Nineteen days out of Sasebo, in a fog so dense that nothing, not even Mt. Rainier, was visible, the troopship docked in Seattle.

Ten hours later in a taxi on the way to the airport, Captains Augustus Bedford Forrest and Benjamin Franklin Pierce nursed a fifth of whiskey. At the airport, everything was fogged in, so they went to the cocktail lounge.

As they sat there at the bar, it all seemed unreal. Two people who had been very important to each other were now almost totally preoccupied with thoughts of other people, and their conversation had become sparse and even a little stilted.

"We don't seem to be acting like Swampmen," observed Duke.

"I guess not, but I don't feel like it. It's just as well."

"Probably."

"Flight 401 for Pendleton, Salt Lake City, Denver and Chicago," blared the loud-speaker.

During the early morning hours, with the moon shining on the snow-covered Rockies, the stewardess addressed the former Swampmen, "I'll have to ask you gentlemen to put away that bottle."

"Sorry, miss," apologized Hawkeye. "We sort of don't know any better."

An hour later the stewardess spoke again to Captain Augustus Bedford Forrest. "Sir, if you don't put away that bottle, I'll have to ask the Captain to come back and speak to you."

218

"That'll be fine, ma'am. We'd be proud to meet him! My buddy here's a Captain, too."

Hawkeye grabbed the bottle and put it away. "Never mind your Captain, honey," he promised. "I'll take care of mine."

At 6:00 A.M., in the men's room of Midway Airport in Chicago, Duke and Hawkeye finished the jug and threw it in a trash can. They were too excited to be drunk. The flight to Atlanta was announced. Duke put his arm around Hawkeye.

"I'll see y'all some time, you goddamned Yankee. Stay loose!"

"Helluva place to end an interesting association, Doctor," said Hawkeye Pierce, "but it's been nice to have known you."

Dr. Augustus Bedford Forrest boarded the plane for Atlanta, where he was met by a big girl and two little ones. Six hours later the valedictorian of the class of 1941 at Port Waldo High School and two small boys watched Dr. Benjamin Franklin Pierce disembark from a Northeast Airlines Convair in Spruce Harbor, Maine.

The larger of the two boys jumped into his father's arms and inquired, "How they goin', Hawkeye?"

"Finest Kind," replied his father.